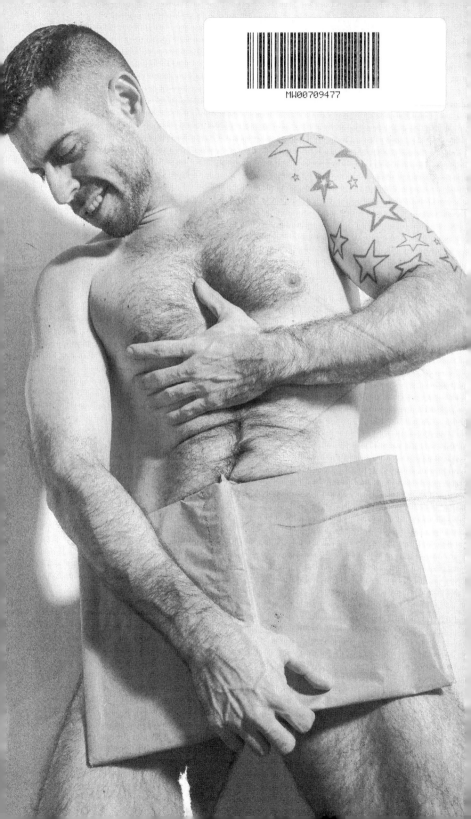

Erotica

EROTICA
BRIANCENTRONE

FEATURING ART BY
TERRY BLAS, ALAN ILAGAN, LUKE KURTIS, & ROB ORDONEZ

NEW LIT
SALON
PRESS

Erotica

Published by New Lit Salon Press, 2014
© 2014 New Lit Salon Press

Cover design by Brian Centrone and luke kurtis
Cover photograph and frontispiece by Rob Ordonez
Art direction and design by luke kurtis

"Mates" originally appeared in *Ultimate Gay Erotica 2007*, Alyson Books, 2007
"Lost" originally appeared in *Treasure Trail: Erotic Tales of Pirates on the High Seas*, Alyson Books, 2007
"Team Player" originally appeared in *Fast Balls: Erotic Tales of America's Favorite Pastime*, Alyson Books, 2007
"Making the Grade" originally appeared in *Brief Encounters: 69 Hot Gay Shorts*, Cleis Press, 2011
"Boracay" originally appeared in *THIS Literary Magazine*, March/April 2011

This collection of stories is a work of fiction. All characters are fictionalized. Any resemblance to those living or dead is purely coincidental.

New Lit Salon Press
Carmel, NY

Print ISBN 978-0-9885512-5-1
eBook ISBN 978-0-9885512-3-7

www.newlitsalonpress.com

Also by New Lit Salon Press

I Voted for Biddy Schumacher: Mismatched Tales from the Mind of Brian Centrone

Retrospective by Michael Tice

Southern Gothic: New Tales of the South

Also by Brian Centrone

An Ordinary Boy

Many thanks to Sandi, Claudia, and Colin for helping me edit these stories over the years, and to Alyson, Cleis, and *THIS* for publishing them.

Thanks to luke kurtis, Terry Blas, Alan Ilagan, and Rob Ordonez for your wonderful artwork. You are all incredible artists and I am honored to showcase your extraordinary work alongside mine.

TABLE OF CONTENTS

OOPS, I DIDN'T KNOW I
COULDN'T WRITE ABOUT SEX

D.H. Lawrence got in trouble over it. Anne Rice used a pen name to write it. E.L. James made a fortune off it. No one can deny that sex sells, yet it remains controversial. The mere mention of erotica sends literary noses pointed toward the heavens in a triumphant stance of superiority. For the majority of the literary world, erotica is not literature at all.

The truth is that some believe erotica is cheap. They dismiss it with other genre writing like Sci Fi or Romance. Many see these types of stories as inferior to scholarly or academic works. I disagree. I won't argue that some erotica is pure smut, merely words to get off by, but not all, and certainly not mine. I believe that there is such a thing as "literary erotica," and I consider my work to fall into that category. Why? Because I write erotic stories the way I write any fiction. I use the building blocks of literature to craft and develop tales which seek for more than just to lube a reader up. My stories aren't about sex. They feature sex, yes, and prominently—that's the nature of erotica—but they are always about something more: love, relationships, self-discovery.

However, while highbrow authors and critics refuse to acknowledge the idea that erotic writing can contain all the elements cherished in their canon of traditional stories, they often overlook the simple fact that many of the writers they hold in esteem have written so-called "trash" themselves. Sex in stories is not a new concept. Hell, sex is all over the

Bible. But what is perceived as a sex scene, or erotica, or pornography is what can easily separate the elite from the rubbish.

So much of my writing career has been overshadowed by the few erotic stories I have published. Often times, this has caused me to ask myself why I didn't publish my erotica under a pen name like so many authors do. There were two reasons for that. The first reason was that I didn't want my first major publication to have a fabricated name on it; a name I didn't identify with. The second reason was that when I was in college I wrote a sex column for the campus newspaper. When it was pitched, I had wanted to write the column under a pen name, but my adviser would not agree to that. She felt that I should stand behind my work, not hide behind a faux name. And while that ideal is questionable at times, it stuck with me. As a writer, I have always wanted the freedom to write what I feel I need to write. And if I am going to write something, then it has to be only I that claims ownership of it.

Still, I was dismissed quite frequently. People wrongly assumed that everything I wrote and published was erotic. I was pigeonholed into a stereotype I was beginning to resent. Often, I had to make judgment calls about listing my publications on resumes for employment. My erotic works were my sole, significant publications. Would I be judged unfairly? This quandary has plagued me for years. So why would I want to collect my erotic works and expose myself to ever more misjudgment? Why follow my debut novel, *An Ordinary Boy*, with a collection of erotic stories? Because I am proud of my work. My erotica is some of the best writing I have ever done. Also because I want to show the world that erotica can be literary. It doesn't have to be only about cheap sex.

I will admit, as I often have, that I didn't intend to enter into the business of writing about sex. I fell into it quite by chance. As many readers may know, my first piece of erotic fiction was "Mates." I had never intended for this piece to be an erotica story. Once I had finished writing it, I thought that the sex, which was an important element of the plot, was more than what one might find in your average short story. This made me think it might find a good home in a gay erotic anthology. And I was right. Alyson, the publishers who I credit for the start of my career, loved my writing. I appeared in three consecutive erotic anthologies in the same year. I was, as they say, on a roll.

For an emerging writer, the idea of being published in a major publication with international distribution supersedes all thoughts of snobbery from the literary community. And of course, for a new gay writer, opportunities to publish can be limited. At the beginning of my career, journals and anthologies featuring gay writing were starting to diminish. Submission calls for gay literary fiction were scarce. But there was never a shortage of erotica calls to be had. Erotica was my first break into the business, and I was grateful to have that break. I was proud of my achievements and even boasted about them. After all, I was a paid writer who was in demand. But even though I had success, I knew erotica wasn't where I wanted to stay. I had more to write, other tales to tell.

As a writer—not a gay writer, not an erotic writer, not a genre writer, but as a writer—I will continue to tell the stories I feel need to be told. They won't all deal with the same issues, won't all be in the same genre, won't all appeal to the same readers. And that is okay. There is more than one way to tell a story, and there is more than one type of story to tell. If that story happens to get you off while reading it, well, then, good.

MATES

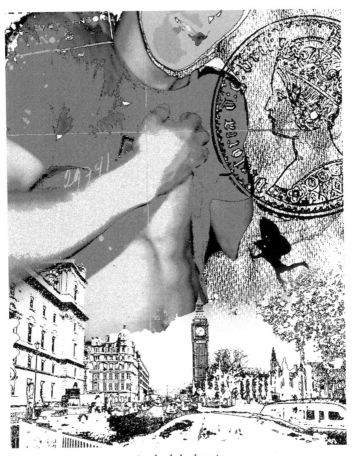

Art by luke kurtis

The door shut with a click signaling it was locked—safe. I looked at Danny and got instantly hard. He had already moved through the room, lowering all the blinds and removing pieces of his clothing. I laughed at his eagerness and sauntered over to the uncomfortable bed. I kicked off my shoes and sat down, the old, coarse, discolored spread giving way to my hasty plop. My eyes roamed over his half-naked body. I took him in, absorbing all of him in my mind. He was tall and lean, almost gangly, but not quite. His head was shaved and his smile was wide, he wore glasses, round and thick, like Coke bottles. His plaid boxers, too big on his frail body, were the only fabric left on him. Danny walked towards me, taking his erect shaft in his left hand, slowly beating it. He closed the gap between us, his foreskin pushed back, ready for me. I stared into his eyes—that long hard stare that connects two men who are about to have sex. It lasted only an instant before I swallowed him whole. I kept my eyes fixed on his face so I could see his expression as I gave him what he had been longing for. Danny moaned. He had never had it so good and I had never had it so uncut.

It was my last night in England. I had spent the summer after graduation studying abroad. My first time in the UK proved to be both eye opening and life changing. I began to see the world in a new light. Everything I had gathered about how the world worked was now replaced by a whole new understanding. I was enlightened and re-nationalized. I was also on a mission—not only to learn, but also to experience the culture, the country, and the men—oh god, the men! England hosted a bevy of hot blokes, all fit and all sexually interested. My plan was set, I knew my mission: to have an English fellow before returning to America.

I released Danny's member from my tight-lipped grasp and examined his meat. I was fascinated with it, tugging the extra skin back and forth, amusing myself, arousing him. Together we slipped the boxers off of his thin waist and he stepped out of them. This gave me a chance at his balls, which were already tight with excitement. I ran my hand through his pubic hair, savoring every inch of his maleness. It was wonderful, *he* was wonderful—foreskin was wonderful.

XXX

I had been flirting with men for weeks, teasing them, turning them on, but I never got to go all the way with any of them. I began to get frustrated. I hadn't jerked off since landing in England weeks ago, and I was ready to blow a huge load. I consoled myself; there were more men, and still London. I would surely score some British arse in London. My first night out in the city I hit a club near my hotel. The great thing about London nightlife, or London in general, is that you don't have to travel far to find what you like. Staying in Piccadilly Circus provided a rather nice opportunity to be in the center of all things, putting me close by to SoHo— London's gay ghetto. With so many varying gay nightclubs and bars in close proximity to each other, SoHo is a gay man's wet dream. The men of London were amazing—fit, well dressed, gorgeous. My eyes went wild canvassing one bloke to the next. I was like a kid in a candy store, except the store was a gay nightclub and the candy was cock.

My store of choice was a corner nightclub that hosted

several bar areas and a few well-placed dance floors. I decided to post myself at the back bar since I had done the front earlier that evening while having drinks with a friend, and found myself engaged in the most tantalizing eye-sex with a passing stranger. He was tall, dark, and extremely sexy. His eyes bored right through me and I was almost positive I would cream just by the intense glance he was giving me.

XXX

I was ready—I removed my own clothes and lay down on the bed taking Danny with me. The spread felt rough beneath my soft skin and slightly scratched me as I adjusted my body to the weight I was now supporting. Danny removed his glasses and meticulously placed them on the nightstand beside us. I wrapped my arms around Danny and ran my hands down his bare back. I followed his curvature until I found his ass, round and smooth, like the rest of him. He went in to kiss me and I caught the smell of booze that lingered on his breath. The scent drove me wild. In the short time I had been in England I had come to adore the smell of booze on a man's breath. How couldn't I? They all reeked of it.

Our lips touched. I parted mine for Danny's probing tongue and for the next five minutes we did nothing but make out. I was gone, taken away by the best kissing I have ever experienced. Danny's lips, full and soft, were sensual. They gently caressed mine and as both our lips moved in synch with each other there was never a moment of roughness or awkwardness. Our lips were a perfect fit. They moved together like a well-rehearsed dance, always in step and always in time. It was during this moment of the night that I began to develop feelings for my British bloke. Our bodies melted together and I knew I never wanted to leave this boy; I had found the one.

Finally the dance ended and our lips broke apart. "That was wonderful," I whispered.

"You make it easy," was Danny's response. Smiling at me, my lover worked his way down to my stiffened cock. It throbbed in anticipation. When those beautiful lips of his grazed my erection, I was in heaven.

XXX

Angels danced around to bad music in ordinary briefs and military boots. Let the truth be known, as England appears to be about a decade behind in musical taste, their dancing ability is really fucking lacking. I watched the body glitter glisten off of sweaty go-go boys atop the bar, the pink and blue gel lights catching their false-feathered wings. I attempted to focus on the angels' snug briefs, but the uncomfortable appearance of their body movements was rather a distraction. I moved further into the bar. It was full, too full, and more guys kept coming in. I was positive the fire code was being broken; then again, I wasn't sure what the fire code was in London. I planned on walking through the bar and into one of the dance floor areas until it thinned out a bit. Before I even got half way through I spotted him. He had been following me with his eyes as I forced my way through the throngs of men. He smiled coyly and his eyes twinkled with possibility. I smiled back. I had only a few seconds to decide whether I wanted to continue on my path and see what my other options might be or go over to this guy and chat him up. I went over.

XXX

I closed my eyes and titled my head back. Danny was good; for a guy who was relatively inexperienced, he was damn good. Never once did I have to instruct him on what to do. He knew; instinctively, he knew. As Danny worked on my cock, I started to wonder about the student who would be taking my room in the fall. Would they have any idea that two men were having sex in the bed they would be sleeping in? Would they care if they found out? Would it freak them out? My thought process was beginning to get me excited. The idea of engaging in something taboo and forbidden heated me up. Danny must have sensed this because he started to work my cock even harder. The boy was turning out to be the best blow of my life. Danny shifted directions slightly and headed south for my balls. He scoped my left nut up with the curl of his tongue, rolling it back and forth before inhaling it into his mouth. By body trembled and convulsed uncontrollably. Without knowing it, the boy had found my spot. My eyes writhed in their sockets. Danny had to stop and ask if I was okay, all I could do was nod and gesture for him to continue.

XXX

Maybe I should have continued, I thought, as I stood next to this handsome stranger. He was older, very mature and very grey on top. More salt-n-pepper, rather. *I always stop too soon*, I kept thinking as this older sport and I played smiley faces with each other.

"Are you British?" I asked, in hopes that tonight I would finally land my bloke.

"Excuse me?" The music was too loud; he hadn't heard what I said.

He turned his ear to me; I leaned in closer to him and repeated myself. He shook his head no.

"I'm Canadian."

Damn!

"I was looking for a British guy," I said bluntly, shrugging my shoulders. "Are you uncut?" I followed up with.

"No."

"But you're Canadian."

He shrugged. "The country goes back and forth on that. There are times when cutting is in and times when it's not." He put the drink he was holding to his lips and took a gulp. The ice in the glass jostled; the light brown liquid slipping back to the bottom when he was done.

I moved in closer to listen to him speak. Men kept pushing into me as they passed on the way to the bar or the door.

My stranger took notice and patted the empty window ledge beside him where he had taken up residence long before I arrived.

"It's getting too crowded in here. You should take a seat, get out of the way."

We were now close enough to talk without shouting, though a degree of projection was still called for.

"So why are you here?" I asked, sliding past a huddle of guys and sitting next to him.

"Business. I'm a war correspondent. I've been in the Middle East for the last few months, but I was told to come to London to cover the British end of it. Why are you here?"

"I'm doing a summer study."

He nodded.

XXX

I was sure I was going to cum. More than sure. If Danny didn't stop what he was doing he was going to get an unexpected face full of my load. I gently pushed away and propped myself up on the bed.

"Come here," I beckoned softly.

He followed my command.

We kissed again. I could taste myself on him. Still locked with Danny, I reached over to the nightstand and felt around for the only condom I had. Grabbing it, I drew it up close to show him. He said nothing. I gave him a quick kiss. We moved into position.

XXX

I shifted on the hard window ledge. I was being asked for at least the fifth time if I wanted to go back to his hotel.

"I shouldn't," I replied.

"What are you scared of?" He looked at the remainder of his drink then placed it aside.

"Nothing, I just don't know if that's something I want to do yet."

The truth was I really wanted to go back to this guy's hotel and have him fuck me. But I didn't want to rush. I needed to take my time.

"How about a drink then?"

"Sure."

He stopped a waiter, ordered a glass of wine and turned to me.

"Screwdriver."

The waiter raised his eyebrows and shook his head slightly.

"He wants a Vodka Orange," my stranger clarified.

The waiter noted the drinks and headed off.

"It's what they call Screwdrivers over here."

I raised my eyebrows in fascination while thoughts whirled around in my head. It had been no more than twenty minutes since I met this guy but I was very attracted to him. He had that distinguished look. Very relaxed, laid back and content. You would never be able to tell that my decision to go home with him was any more significant than buttering popcorn, but it was. The more I spent talking with him the more I wanted to go with him. Something, however, kept telling me to hold back.

We continued to chat, talking about nothing really at all. I was attempting to stretch time, and as it dragged on, no drinks ever showed.

I kept watching the crowd. More men kept coming in while the angels on top of the bar had somehow turned into sailor boys. The waiter that took our order passed through the herd of men a few times never once with an acknowledgment.

"I think he might have forgotten us."

I agreed.

"I have alcohol at my place. The mini fridge is stocked with it. Everything's on the company of course. We could go back and have some."

"I don't even know your name," I stated in an attempt to delay things even more, though by now my ridgid pole was ready to accept the offer.

"Nick."

My eyes widened a bit. "Really? That's interesting."

"Why so?" He looked curious.

I leaned further towards him. "I had my cards read one Pride back in New York. The lady came up with three names that would be significant. One was Nick."

"See then," he said coyly, cocking his head, "it was meant to be."

I smiled. "Maybe." I guess the sixth time was the charm or perhaps it was the immense strain in my jeans; either way, my resolve was lost.

"Okay," I grinned.

"Okay?" He searched for an explanation.

"Okay, let's go back to your hotel."

Nick smiled. "Okay."

XXX

Danny helped me roll on the condom. He lay down softly on the bed. Tossing his legs up over my shoulders, I told him to relax as I glided myself in him. Hot and tight; I thrust forward again and again. Danny's eyes remained closed, blank expression on his face. The only cues I got that he was enjoying what I was doing to him were the delicate moans that he allowed to occasionally escape from between his supple lips.

I pulled out, not wanting to finish too soon. Once again my back was against the rough spread with Danny's face buried deep between my legs. I held out as long as I could but the sensations that ran through my body were far more powerful. My panting got louder and louder.

"I'm going to cum," I let out.

Danny's mouth held on tight as I erupted, spewing one powerful load after another of my seed for him to have. He swallowed as much as he could, the excess falling back out and onto my recently freed cock.

After Danny had cum, we lay in each other's arms for a brief while, kissing. I wanted the moment to last forever, but it wasn't possible. Danny had to go, and in the morning, so did I. The whole experience almost seemed unfair. Perhaps if it felt more like a one night stand instead of an actual connection, seeing him go wouldn't have been so crushing.

I hurriedly dressed myself as Danny made sure he looked put-together. We kissed several more times; the bloke was insatiable.

"I'll never forget you," he whispered.

My heart was stolen in that moment.

Watching him slip through the gates of the college and into the dark of night I felt, for the first time in the entire trip, that I lost a piece of myself.

XXX

Nick took my virginity that night in his hotel room. He didn't know it and I never told him. It was a one-time thing and I was fine with that. I never once regretted it. I did regret, however, that I had a week left in the UK and I had yet to have my bloke.

The week passed too quickly and I found myself sitting in the college bar saying goodbye to all the great new friends I had made. It was a bittersweet event to say the least and I had no plans of vacating the spot until it was absolutely necessary. A crashing mix of jukebox jingles and last time conversations vibrated off the walls. Everything was a buzz.

"I've wanted to meet you for a while, but I never come into the bar," this guy I had just met said to me while we were alone at a table. A member of staff I had befriended introduced us.

"You should, it's fun in here." I nodded my head.

"It's always too loud."

"We could go back to my room. Not loud there," I flirted out of habit.

"That would be nice. Do you want to go now?"

I was taken aback. I looked at him questioningly. He asked again.

"Sure, Danny, we can go back to my room now."

LOST

Art by Terry Blas

"This is a really nice place you got," this 'Pirate Pete' said when we entered my home.

"Thanks," I mumbled, looking behind me before I closed the door, making sure no one had seen us. "It's been in the family for years."

"You live alone then?"

I looked directly at him for the first time since we met as I had arranged. "Yes." I switched on the lights. "I'm the end of the line," I attempted to sound whimsical. "The end of a long line..."

We stood quietly for a few minutes. I wasn't sure what to do next. This wasn't anything I had ever done before and, to be honest, I was scared to death.

"Do you mind if I take a seat?" my pirate broke the silence.

"Oh, of course!" I was flustered. "Do you want a drink?"

"Some rum, if you have it? Just to set the mood," he winked.

His remark made me laugh, which helped me to calm down. Taking a deep breath, I went over to the bar and poured us both a generous glass.

Handing him the rum, I sat next to him. Our thighs grazed and a shot of electricity surged through me. I tingled in places I never thought another man could make me tingle.

"This is your first time, isn't it?" he remarked, sipping his drink.

Clearly he was picking up on my sheepishness. It couldn't be helped. I wasn't gay, after all, and here I was, bringing a man dressed in a costume back to my home just so I could know what it was like to be fucked hard by a pirate.

I nodded silently, looking at the dark liquid in my glass.

"We don't have to go through with this if you don't want to. I won't be offended. You just seem really uncomfortable."

I looked at him again. He had gone all out for the part. Tights, head wrap, ruffled shirt and vest, boots, gold hoop earrings, a sword (fake, I think) and even an eye patch. I sighed heavily and opened my mouth to speak. Before I could get a word out, Pirate Pete leaned in quickly and covered my mouth with his. Our lips met and his stubble felt rough against my smooth skin. I dissolved into his kiss instantly and let myself be carried away. My pirate pulled away and smiled as I attempted to stay connected.

"I knew you would like it and get into it with a little help," he laughed.

He was right. All I needed was a little push. Perhaps I was more like my great-great-great-great-great grandfather than I thought. After all, he was the reason I was doing this.

Pirate Pete leaned in for another kiss; this time I was ready for it, wanted it and took control of it. This second kiss was harder and more passionate. It lasted longer and while our lips got to know each other, so did our hands. Our bodies fit tightly as he ran his hands down me and I got to feel just how hard this pirate was. He pressed against me, straining, and I knew for sure that was exactly what I wanted and needed. Any doubt I had was gone. I was about to share the same experience my grandfather had all those years ago. This is what I was after, why I found my pirate. Before the night was over I would share more with my grandfather than just his name.

James Gloust was a famous explorer. He kept extensive

journals of his travels that have been coveted by museums, historians and scholars for centuries. And though his journals don't differ much from any other explorer's, what makes my grandfather stand out above the rest is what he doesn't say. The part of his time at sea that has never been recorded is the short period he spent lost. No one seems to know why he never wrote about this particular time, or, if he had, when and where those missing entries disappeared.

The truth is that his questionable time did not go unrecorded. My grandfather did in fact write about his time lost at sea. But the nature of what happened to him was seen as so taboo that my family kept it hidden away, claiming never to be in possession of these highly sought-after documents.

For all of my life I, too, believed these journal entries did not exist or were lost. I only discovered the truth after inheriting the family archives, passed down from generation to generation. Losing both my parents, I became the last member of the Gloust line. I was left with no other choice but to bear this secret burden thrust upon me.

Needless to say, I was shocked. Not simply because these entries actually existed and were in my family's possession, but because of what was written. Reading them, I couldn't help but understand why they were made to disappear. What troubled me wasn't the tale my grandfather told, but the need I developed—more than a need, a desire, an obsession to fully understand his emotions and actions that all started that stormy night in the Pacific…

XXX

I was feeling a bit queasy as the boat rocked to and fro. Housed in the bowels of the ship, my sleeping chamber was particularly ideal for discomfort and annoyance, and, as on this night, the rowboat had not been brought on board from that morning's exploration and was left to trail from the ship—the crew and Captain being the laziest of all seamen I've ever encountered—and was banging up against the walls around me. Taking it upon myself, I emerged from my chamber and fought my way on deck. The sea was troubled that night and I should have paid it some mind, but all I could consider was being well rested for the next day's adventures. Making my way to port side I attempted to raise the tiny boat myself. Of course, not being experienced in such things, I could not. Instead I decided I would try to alter its position so that it would cease its attack on the side of my chamber. This time I was positive I could accomplish my task but as luck would have it—and I can only say that now—the sea grew angry, sending a swell of water that rocked the ship, causing me to stumble over.

Before I knew what was amiss, I was struggling to seek shelter in the rowboat. In achieving this I realized that the rope, due to my efforts, had come undone and I was being carried away in a direction no compass could determine. I held on to the seats for dear life as the sea carried me away through the night. I was sure I would never see my native England again and, even worse, that I would be leaving behind my fiancée, whom I was due to marry upon my return from my expedition of the islands in the Pacific. It was not until the break of light that I dared to look up and in doing so, released my precious hold, for land was dead ahead.

Even I could not express the joy that bubbled inside of me as my rowboat washed up on shore. I snaked my way onto the dry sand that clung to my wet attire. I cared nothing except for the fact that I was alive.

After regaining myself (I must sheepishly confess that took a great deal of time), I got up from my haven of sand and took a good look about the island. Fear began to set. I knew not where I was, nor did the crew on my ship. Could they locate me? Would they locate me? Panic took over and I moved further into the brush in search of survival aids. Would there be food for me to get by? If there was any form of animal on this island besides the birds that soared overhead, I could not find tracks. I thought for sure my life would end on that island. Nevertheless, it was not until I reached about the middle of the thicket that my path crossed with destiny.

A rumble and crush. A swoosh and snap. An "arrrgh" and a sword. He stood before me, chest puffed and exposed, eyes squinted, and thighs firmly set. His clothes were in tatters and he wore a stained strip of cloth around his head, his long, dark hair, dirty and matted, flowing beneath.

I thought my heart would stop! Paralyzed with fear, I was under his surrender. He pushed his sword in as far as it would go before piercing my body and scowled again.

"The name's Radley. Cap'n Drake Radley. What business have you on me island?"

I stammered and he pushed the sword in harder.

"I'm lost," I spat out. He released some of the pressure. "I was thrown overboard in a violent storm..." I stumbled over the rest, unsure of how much detail he actually desired. It must have sufficed, for he lowered his sword completely and began to laugh like a mad man.

"So yer shipwrecked, are ya?" he finally got out.

I didn't think disputing the difference between being shipwrecked and thrown overboard would particularly sit well with this swashbuckler, so I decided against calling it to his attention. Instead I merely nodded.

After his cackling ended he eyed me with a look that made my skin crawl. A sneer spread across his face.

"I'm not here for trouble," I said, trying to put on an air of confidence.

"What trouble ye be talking about then?"

I gulped hard. "I would like to get back to my ship. If you

can be of any assistance, I'm sure I can arrange a monetary award..."

Drake looked at me hard as if I had offended him greatly. He growled again and sprang forward, grabbing hold of me and pulling my body, rigid with fear, close to him.

"Now listen here, matey, I don't need yer gold and I don't need to help ya get off me island, ya see? I'm in control here and whatever I says goes."

He shoved me to the ground and stood over me, one foot perched on my chest.

"Please," I began to mutter over and over again, sounding like a terrified child crying for his mother.

The pirate just laughed, digging the heel of his boot into my chest harder before releasing his pressure, giving me a little kick on the side.

"Get up," he ordered.

I struggled to my feet, trying to steady my legs. I was aware I was wobbling with fright and it would do me better if I put on an air of bravery, but for the life of me, and at this point I was positive there wasn't much of it left, I couldn't do anything but cower.

"Now that ye be on me island, there be some rules to follow."

I nodded vigorously, not wanting to upset him.

"First, yer mine for as long as ye lasts here. And second, there's been nobody on this here island for a long time." He looked me up and down. His gold earrings glistened in the sunlight as he did so. "A man can get very tense when his needs aren't met..." He wet his coarse lips with his tongue.

I knew for sure that I was about to be devoured like mutton, but I hadn't quite realized how.

"Ye understand those two things there and ye be fine. Now get movin'." He pointed his sword at me again and I forced my legs to start walking.

I tripped over roots and brush as he forced me along an unclear path. I dared not ask where we were headed.

The sun poured down on us as we made our way. The palms did little to cool me as they should have, but my body was tense and my heart pounded feverishly. Sweat dripped down me, soaking my sea logged clothes even more.

We seemed to be walking without any chance of stopping. There was either no end to this island or, as I began to expect when the morning sun shifted positions for afternoon and finally early evening, I was being led in a deliberate circle, sword tip pinned to my back.

When I thought I couldn't carry on anymore I was ordered to take a sharp turn and I fought my way through a heavy gate of trees, finally coming to a clearing. There in the distance docked on shore was one of the most amazing ships I had ever seen, and raised high above it was a Jolly Roger flowing in the breeze.

The sight sent more terror than what already surged through me. Seeing this flag brought me to my knees. What I would find once on that ship was a thought I couldn't bear.

"There's me ship. The Molly. Ain't she a beaut?" he whistled.

I nodded silently, eyes fixed on that black piece of cloth. "Do you always fly your flag when you're not on board?" I dared to query.

"Lest it be known where people are trespassing..." He looked over at me and cocked his head. "Why ye be curious?"

"Are you really the only one on this island? Have you no one on your ship?" My terror was forcing me to speak against my better judgment. I knew my questioning would anger him, but I had to know whether or not I was being led to a gang of bloodthirsty pirates where I would undoubtedly meet my fate. In all my years at sea I had never come across these barbaric men, but knew fully their capabilities. The stories of their attacks were known and feared by any good-natured soul who sailed the seas.

Drake growled at me. Just as I suspected, my words had set him off.

"I'm the only one on this here island. And like I said, things can get pretty tense on yer own..." Drake shoved his foot into my back and I fell on my chest. "I was goin' ter wait til we got aboard, but I thinks yer wantin' ter know what I mean when I says I'm in charge."

Drake turned me over with his foot and ran it down the length of my body until he reached my crotch. He toyed with it, putting just enough pressure to arouse it against my will.

I looked up at him for the briefest of moments, catching the lust that had filled his eyes before looking down to where I was growing steadfast at an alarming rate. Despite my terror, I couldn't help but feel a tinge of heat searing through me.

The pirate removed his foot and, pushing at my bottom slightly, said, "Get up and strip."

I lay there quite still for a moment before his foot jostled my bottom again, this time with more force.

I was on my feet in no time, but the removal of my clothes was slow going. This angered him, as he pulled at me again, ripping off what was left.

"That's more like it," he sneered, wetting his lips again.

He examined my naked body, turning me this way and that. Oh, how I thought I'd never live that moment down, if I lived at all.

"Excited, are ya?" Drake laughed, eyeing my rigid pole. "Good, good. That makes two of us."

With a swift motion he released what had to be the biggest cock I had ever seen through a slit in his worn trousers. Thick and veiny, his battering ram pulsated as he bobbed it up and down.

"Get down here and clean it," he ordered.

I obeyed without hesitation for fear of what might become of me if I did not follow his demands.

My bare knees scraped against the dry sand and foliage beneath me. I stared directly at the beast before my eyes, seeming even more monstrous up close. The concept of what was supposed to be done was the only thing I had to go on, never being with a man in this way. Closing my eyes I opened my mouth and preened forward. The pirate's giant timber slid in, his extra skin moving back as his bulbous head hit the back of my throat. The scent of his manliness hit me like a falling mast, my nose buried deep in his scruffy pubes. I gagged reflexively, but my captor only thrust further, snarling and moaning as he did.

Tears began to well in my eyes and I thought I would pass out from lack of breath, but to my surprise, I began to get used to his torpedoing. Eventually his cock was sliding in and out with no problems at all.

I was leaking heavily by this point and desperately wanted to relieve myself. I couldn't quite understand my body's reaction to my pillaging, nor did I have time to attempt to make sense of it.

Allowing me a breath, the pirate removed his mass fully.

Relaxing back on my heels, I took a gulp of air.

"We're not done," he informed me, whipping out his full, hairy balls. "These need tending to as well," he smirked, grabbing my head and pushing me back for a second round of tongue bathing.

Weighty as coconuts, I began work on his balls, licking and sucking as he instructed. He became more vocal with this venture, telling me what to do and if he liked it.

"That's it there, Matey, just like that," he groaned as I mouthed his hairy nuts. "Now get back to me log." He pulled away from me slightly so he could get a proper angle to shove his massive meat back down my throat. Again he moaned, closing his eyes and tilting his head back. "Yer better than any of my cabin boys…and crew for that matter," he chuckled. "I used to make them stand around me on deck and one by one me men would swab me cock with their spit till I was nice and slick. Just right to roger the young lad or two we had sailing with us."

Morally I was appalled by what he was telling me and what he was making me do, but sexually I was more excited than ever.

Drake seemed to go into some sort of trance, as if remembering these moments, but he wasn't in it for long before jerking his cock back out of my mouth and giving me the dirtiest look yet.

"I think I'm nice and slick now…"

No matter how hard my own cock got, I knew I wasn't ready for what was about to happen.

He turned me around, making me support myself on all fours. Kneeling behind me, he positioned his mast at my never-opened hatch. I could hear him hacking up spit, then felt it wet my hole. He rubbed it in and around with his thumb and pointer finger before spitting again and going through the same routine. When he was done, he placed the head of his cock against my lubed entrance. The feeling sent a series of reactions through my body. My stomach sank with nerves and fear while my cock jerked with excitement and anticipation. He pushed in, the head prying open my tight ring. I took a deep breath and waited. Without any sense of care he rammed the rest home once the fat head had been swallowed. I let out a scream and he laughed, pounding away, his heavy balls slapping against my ass cheeks. Drake grabbed on to my hips for a harder, faster pound. "Oh fuck," he cried. "Nice and tight. Just the way I like it."

I whimpered along as he stretched me out, my cock leaking like a sinking ship.

"It's been so long," he muttered roughly as he bottomed out, stayed in me for a few seconds, then withdrew fully only to slam his wood back in at full force.

The pain was subsiding and I was getting used to the feeling of having my insides turned out. In fact, I was beginning to enjoy his barrage of my hole so much so that I began to back up against him, trying to match his thrust.

"Yeah, get into it," he moaned, "ride me pirate cock."

Like I had gotten used to, I did what he commanded and before long I was the one doing all the fucking, bouncing off his hard pelvis as I rode his pole.

Jerking my body up, he pulled me with him while he lay on the ground, me on top. I bounced up and down, loving the feeling on his invasion. I cried out myself, causing Drake to take action again, matching my motions. He thrust up as I down and soon we were both ready to explode. He spun me around on his stick just in time for me to unleash a load of cum all over his ripped abs. The act alone set him off his rocker and with a grunt resembling that of a wild beast he shot his own load, swearing and moaning as he did.

I collapsed onto him, our bodies sweaty from the hot sex. His chest rose and fell as he tried to regain a normal breathing pattern. My head rested on his developed pecs and I could hear and feel his heartbeat. It was pounding in him as hard as he had pounded in me.

I was beginning to calm down when he violently threw me off without warning. My body hit the ground hard. I winced from the impact.

"Now get up and dressed," he ordered.

I did as he said, waiting for his next command.

"Come. I'll show yer me Molly." He slapped my back and moved ahead towards the shore.

I followed behind, careful not to trip over any of the brush that rustled beneath my feet. By the time I reached

43

the ship, he was already on board. He gave me a hand up, beaming from ear to ear.

"How do'ya like her?" His demeanor had changed from the gruff pirate I had experienced on land. He became a little boy showing off a new toy.

"She's something," I said, meaning it. The ship was impressive. From the angle of the bough, the entire horizon spanned across. The starry night appeared endless while the moon delicately dipped itself into the Pacific.

"I'll show ya me cabin," he said, coming up behind me. He placed a hand on each of my shoulders, letting them rest there.

A tingle ran up my spine and I tried to keep from quivering. I liked the touch. It was soft, very different from the way he had grabbed me and made me do his bidding. But all of it was confusing me. I didn't know why he made such a switch once we were on his ship and I didn't know why I was beginning to like the contact. I wanted to shake off the feeling I was having.

Turning away from him, I walked in the direction of the cabin. He strode ahead of me, leading the way. I was in complete awe of what I saw. The spoils of piracy had done him wonders. The cabin was decked with luxuries only found on the best ships of Europe. Silks and satins, jewels and crystals, gold and silver, paintings and statues, they all filled the space. It was if I had just walked into the Queen's bedchamber.

He had to notice the expression on my face, for he remarked, "What can I say. I like to live like royalty," then laughed hardily.

I merely nodded.

He came up behind me again, this time pressing his body into mine. I could feel his hard mast straining against my well-worn hatch and a surge of excitement and fear filled me.

"Get on the bed," he whispered in my ear.

As always, I obeyed.

He fucked me softly that second time, both of us falling asleep after it was over. I awoke in the middle of that night to find myself curled up in his strong arms. I moved slightly and he stirred. He turned his head towards me, opening his eyes. Leaning in, he kissed me. I was taken aback. His lips were rough like him, but the kiss was as gentle as a lamb. I loved the way it felt and immediately broke away, moving back.

"Why are you on this island?" I asked trying to slow things down, even more confused than ever by his behavior and my emotions. I couldn't help but wonder how this man came to be on his own.

"Arrr. Now that's a story itself." He turned away. "I was one of the greatest Pirate cap'ns to ever sail the seven seas. There was no port I wasn't feared. Me crew was known to be the most ruthless cutthroats you'd ever shiver to come across. For years we went wherever and took whatever we pleased. But I was always hungry for more. It took its mark on me mates. I began to share less, order them around more. It was me greed that did me in. A mutiny was in order, that was for sure. I knew it would come, and soon. So I did what any great pirate would do: I got rid of them..."

"You mean you killed them?" I shot up. I was startled and dismayed at the thought.

"Nar. I just left them at port. They all went ashore after a long haul and while they were pillaging the village I sailed away. But ye see, all I did after that was come here. I couldn't continue without a crew, no matter how crafty a pirate I be. So I docked on this island waiting for the right time to sail again."

"When will that be?"

"Don't know. Been here for years, I reckon, and still haven't gotten the urge to return. I quite like it."

"But surely you must get lonely?" I couldn't fathom the idea of living an isolated life on an uncharted island. It was preposterous to me.

"A man needs no one but himself for company. You'd do best to learn that. The only thing I have been missing is something nice and tight, and ya fixed that," he winked at me.

I laid back down thinking of all he said. He seemed content with his life on the island, happy to be alone, but I still couldn't grasp it.

Over the next couple of days things began to change. He became softer and the sex became passionate and personal. When we weren't in his bed we were exploring the island. He showed me what fruits to eat and which animals lived on the island. He even put me to work on the ship, explaining how I could sail and tend to a vessel if need be. We talked more and more and soon I began to feel for Drake. When he wasn't being a pirate he was like any other man you would find on the street and wish a good day. And, if I dare say, at times, I even thought he was better. But no matter how fond of him I grew and no matter how much I had come to enjoy having him plunge my depths, every time I spied that flag I couldn't help be reminded that he was a villain, plain and simple. He had to remain exactly what he was, a pirate.

Before I had time to rationalize the situation I had found myself in, fate took another twist. One morning I was on deck for a breath of fresh air. The pleasure I felt from the night's splendors faded quickly. Looking out to sea, my heart sunk. There in the distance, right in front of the rising sun, were the white sails and the bright flapping flags of my ship. Somehow they found where the stormy sea had carried me. All my senses told me I should feel elated to be discovered and rescued, but I was feeling quite forlorn. In the short time

I had been on this island, in the capture of this pirate, I began to see what he saw. Or at least began to understand why he was content with being on his own.

I had lain awake all those nights while he slept beside me and thought how peaceful I felt. The island was calm; there was not a thing to worry about. Everything that was needed was there. It was an escape from the world, one where you didn't have to worry what other people thought or expected of you. You were your own person and capable of enjoying the company of a fellow man in the most intimate of ways without being an outcast of society. It wasn't exactly heaven, but it was some kind of rapture.

I heard footsteps approaching from behind and I turned to see Drake sauntering over in the nude. I gave him a half-hearted smile.

"They found me," I spoke softly. I turned back to look at the ever looming vessel.

Drake neared and looked out over the waters as I was.

"Are you going to put up a fight or let them take me back?" I queried. I needed to know the answer. Deep within me, how he replied weighed heavily.

"Yer not a captive. Yah can come and go as yer please." He walked back into the cabin.

I felt a shattered man. Dressing fully I prepared to leave the ship. Drake remained quiet and out of sight until I was ready to disembark.

"Here," he handed me a lit torch. "It will be easier for them to find you with this."

"Thank you." I looked into his eyes. They had turned stony.

"Now go." With that he was gone.

I trudged my way through the thick and brush until I reached the shoreline. I waved the torch adamantly, the black smoke sending signals of my existence on the island.

The ship got as close as it could, then out came a few men in a rowboat to fetch me and the boat I had vanished on.

"We weren't sure we would find you, Mr. Gloust," the captain said, "but you are definitely worth a try." He smiled brightly.

I put on airs, thanking him repeatedly for his generosity and belief in me.

As the ship rounded the island to get back on course, I thought for sure we would see the Molly, its Jolly Roger flying defensively, but it wasn't there, at least, not on shore. I looked around furiously, for where it had gone I was most determined to discover. And then I saw it, or thought I did. I called to the first mate to lend me his spyglass. Through that long wooden tube, my sighting proved correct. The Molly had set sail once again. Far off in the distance, she glided along the ocean. How she got so far so fast I would not fathom. I felt a mix of joy and loss. For I was sure I would never come across my pirate again, and I knew that once I returned to society I would never experience what I did on the island. Yet for Drake, I knew something had changed and it was I that had changed it. Whatever I came to represent to him, I felt for sure my desertion, if you will, set him on a course back to the living world. Was that good or bad, I couldn't quite determine. He had left his paradise, but perhaps in a need to find another one—a paradise where others existed and where a man did need something more than himself. I knew not what our destinies held. My only hope was that he found what I lost….

X X X

Pete reached between my legs and I spread them, giving my pirate full access. His frilly shirt came off and so did mine. I stroked his bare chest; it was hard and defined with just a hint of hair. I ran my hands down his strong back until I reached the waist of his tights. Yanking on them, Pirate Pete helped me to take them off, then assisted me with mine. While he wore nothing underneath, I had boxers on. He soon shucked those and climbed back up on me. Our rigid cocks rubbed against each other and I swelled with desire. I had to know what it was like to have him inside me. I spread my legs and lifted them so I could wrap them around his waist.

He breathed into my ear, "Oh yeah, baby. You want my pirate cock deep in your hole."

I was so overcome that all I could do was nod.

Pirate Pete bit my ear softly before suckling it. "You ready for my meat?" he asked, positioning himself after slipping on protection and lubing me up.

This time I replied. "Shove your mast in my hatch."

I winced and clenched my teeth to try and handle the pain of being rammed hard for the first time. But as he docked in and out of my port, the pain subsided and the pleasure my grandfather must have felt when Drake rogered him soared through me.

James Gloust never mentioned Drake in any other of his journals, nor did he ever mention being with another man ever again. It could have been a one off. It could have been that what he and Drake shared on that island was so precious to him that he knew he could never replicate it with any other man. Or it could have been that when he returned home from his journeys he settled in to married life and wanted to remain faithful and true to his new wife and children. I can't say for sure, but I can say, knowing what it's like to be fucked hard and passionately by a pirate, going back to anything ordinary seems unfathomable.

TEAM PLAYER

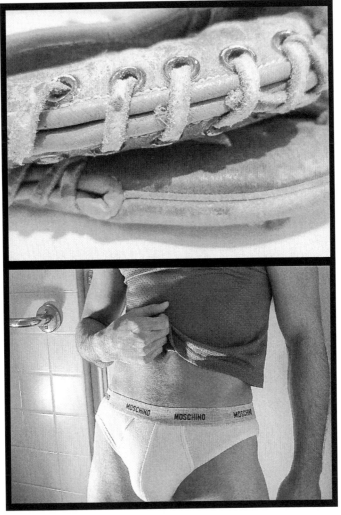

Art by Alan Ilagan

"It's the top of the ninth. Troy Rodriguez has just come up to bat. This is the Houston Ballers' last chance to turn this game around. Will he be able to do it, Chuck?"

"I don't know, Barry. Troy's had a tough season this year. He hasn't been living up to the manager's expectations. A strikeout from him could mean a trade."

"What a change in Rodriguez's playing since he was first signed to the Ballers. He was this team's golden boy."

"That was before he became the playboy he is today. I think all his—how should we say it; the kids at home might be listening—extracurricular activities have really affected his game. I mean here we had a top player who's arguably in baseball's worst slump?"

"I couldn't agree with you more, Chuck. Maybe if Troy spent more time playing on the field then playing the field, he might have led his team to the championship this year instead of the dog house."

"That's a harsh statement, Barry."

"Well, it has to be said."

"There he goes, he's at the plate. Look at that stance; he seems nervous."

"I'd be nervous, too, if this was my last chance."

"Here comes the ball…and…ohhh…strike one."

"Things are not looking good for our boy Troy out there. Two more misses and it's *hasta la vista* for Rodriguez."

"He's shuffling about. Seems like he can't find a good

stance."

"I bet he's just buying time. He knows if he messes this up, that's it for him. He's outta here for good."

"Well, here's his chance for redemption. It's the second pitch…and…strike two! He's behind in the count—exactly where he doesn't want to be right now!"

"One more and he is gone…"

"But you know, Barry, the Ballers aren't totally at a loss with Troy. Their new hitter, Joey Dumbfell, is really proving himself."

"I'm sure Troy must be feeling the choke with that one. His replacement's already starting to sweep him up and out."

"Here's the last pitch, we'll find out soon enough…and he's caught looking—that's it! It's over! Rodriguez lost the game and, most likely, his position with the Houston Ballers."

"The devastation that must be going on right now, not only from our boy Troy, but the whole team, not to mention the coach and manager."

"I'd hate to be in that locker room tonight."

"You said it, Chuck."

XXX

Troy Rodriguez entered the Houston Ballers' locker room with his head down and his guard up. He knew this day was coming and, now that it had finally arrived, he braced himself for the backlash about to come his way.

"Fucking twat, you lost us the chance at the goddamn championship, Rodriguez!" Samson Mills, the third baseman, slammed the locker door shut so hard it bounced back open.

"If you stopped sticking your dick in every cunt that walked by you and put more time into your game, we wouldn't be the laughingstock of the fucking league."

A towel flew across the room, landing at Troy's feet.

He looked up to see who had thrown it. Michael Longbow, the team's starting pitcher, stood at the far end of the room, wearing just his jockstrap. "Use it to wipe up the blood when they're fucking done with you, Rodriguez. You know how I hate a messy locker room."

Troy gazed around to see what the other guys were up to and, more precisely, to see where his next attack would come from. Most of the lads were sulking instead of fuming, choosing to strip from their blue and gray uniforms and shower and change rather than take their wrath out on Troy.

As he stood back from the crowd, Troy noticed one player who seemed totally unfazed by the group's mood. Joey Dumbfell was going about his business of peeling off his snug new uniform with the merriest of attitudes.

Troy could only imagine the bliss that was going through the newbie's mind. Why the fuck wouldn't he be happy? He had come to replace the failing star hitter and tonight, he finally succeeded. Troy would be out by morning and Dumbfell would be the Ballers' next big thing.

"All right boys, listen up," Coach McNara whizzed by. "I know this is a major letdown both personally and professionally, but you can't let this get to you." Coach placed his foot on one of the benches in the middle of the room and leaned on his propped-up knee as he continued his sermon. "There'll be some big changes being made to the team over the next few days—" his eyes that had been roaming the crowd now rested on Troy "—and I want you all to be assured that change brings a better season for the Ballers! Now finish getting ready, have a good rest, and I'll see you all tomorrow for practice."

Coach headed out, stopping by Troy. "In my office when you're dressed."

Troy nodded his head and, when Coach had left, descended further into the locker room.

He sighed deeply as he straddled the bench outside his locker, inhaling the musty, damp, and sweaty scents that clung to the air in the locker room for dear life. It was a familiar smell, one that Troy found both repulsive and comforting, and now he would most likely never get to smell it again.

It was his fault and he knew it. There was no one else to blame but himself. Troy had let his concentration slip. He wasn't training as hard anymore. Maybe he had gotten caught up in all the glory of being the team's golden boy. Troy ignored the comments about him becoming cocky, flippant, and arrogant. And when the press first started in about the various girls he was bedding, he found it humorous. What could he do? He was young and horny. He needed a lot of release from the pressures of playing professional baseball and there never seemed a shortage of chicks who were willing to help him out. Only now it became part of the problem and was half the reason he was getting traded or sacked or whatever the higher ups had in store for him.

Rubbing his face with both hands, Troy sighed deeply before taking a look around the locker room. He was alone. Standing up, he began to strip out of his uniform, kicking off his cleats first, then yanking off his top, followed by sliding down his snug pants, his socks and stirrups coming off with them. Troy kicked at the pile of clothes before plopping back down on the hard wooden bench in only his jockstrap.

"Fuck," he shouted out, banging his fist against the bench. Every muscle in his built body twitched. He was so angry with himself, with the whole situation. He banged the bench again before leaning back on it for a rest.

Troy studied the drop ceiling as he thought more about what led him to this day. He focused on some dark brown stains that spread across a few of the tiles. They were the same color as his nipples, now grown hard from the chill in the room. Remembering the first time he ever lay down on this bench, Troy ran a hand up his naturally bronzed body, feeling every cut of his abs before reaching his nipple. He tweaked it a few times, the feeling arousing him.

When Troy first joined the Ballers, he found the atmosphere in the locker room electrified with sexual tension. Though he had been playing sports since he was a little boy, and every locker room he'd ever been in from adolescence to college had the same bustling tension, the Ballers' felt even more heightened. At first Troy couldn't figure out why and then one day it came to him. It was the grown men, fully aware and fully capable sexually.

He was so eager in those days to be liked, to be considered part of the team that he'd do just about anything to fit in. Being so young and willing to please... Oh, God, did he remember. He remembered all of it, no matter how hard he tried to forget and put it past him. Every attempt to push it away brought him closer to it and instead of facing it he pushed harder to get away from it. But he couldn't. He knew that now. He knew a lot of things now. Worse was that the memories still got to him, still turned him on, just as they were now while he lay on the bench, his free hand inching its way to his excited cock without him even realizing it.

Troy shut his eyes as his strong grip took hold of his own bat. It throbbed in his hand and he applied more pressure to satisfy it. He wanted to free it from the trap of his jockstrap and jerk his dark meat furiously.

He should do it; he needed the release.

Pinching his nipple harder, Troy let a soft moan escape his pouty lips. In one swift move, he freed his cock and pumped fast and hard. His breathing was heavy and his chest rose and fell with each intake and exhalation of breath.

Troy knew he wouldn't last long. His balls were already starting to pull up. He needed this. He needed it so much.

"Well, well, well, what do we have here?"

Troy shot up like a pole vault, his hands ripped from his body and any semblance of orgasm lost.

"Pulling your pud in the locker room again, Troy?" Mills laughed. "I didn't know you still did that."

"I don't," Troy spit out, trying to adjust his position on the bench while stuffing his now soft cock back into his jockstrap.

"That's not what it looks like to us," Longbow chimed in, coming around the corner in just a towel. He was still wet from the showers.

Mills, who was totally in the buff, walked in front of Troy.

"I thought you guys had gone." Troy averted his eyes from Mills' dangling package.

"We were just in the shower getting all nice and clean while you were getting down and dirty." Mills clutched his cock and pulled on it for emphasis.

"I don't think he was getting as dirty as he could, or used to," Longbow winked.

"I don't know what you're talking about." Troy was antsy to get out of the room and more so to get on some clothes. He wasn't sure if he should attempt to make a move or not. He desperately wanted to bolt, but did everything he could to play it cool until he saw an opportunity to escape.

"I think you do," Longbow egged on.

"Come on, Troy, for old time's sake," Mills cooed. "Just like when we were starting out."

"I said I don't know what you're talking about." Troy continued to look away, focusing his gaze on nothing in the distance.

"Don't tell us you don't remember?" Longbow chipped in, coming around the other side of Troy and placing his knee on the bench, his towel spreading open over his muscular thigh.

"How could you forget?" Mills traded grins with his pal. "You loved it when we spit-roasted you."

"Fuck off, Mills!" Troy snapped, jumping up to take on his teammate. He'd had enough. If he didn't act now, he knew he'd find himself in a situation he no longer wanted any part of.

"Now, now, Troy, let's not get testy," Longbow soothed. "We all know you're about to get the sack for sucking on the field. So before you do, why not have a suck in the locker room?"

The players chuckled.

"Yeah, Troy boy. Why not go out with a bang?!"

"A gangbang," Longbow threw in.

"Ooooohhh." Mills and Longbow high-fived each other like a couple of middle schoolers.

"I told you to fuck off." Troy positioned himself, ready for a fight. He stared Mills dead in the eyes, fist raring to go.

"Whoa, whoa. Hold up here, Troy boy," Mills stopped laughing. "We're just being friendly, that's all. We miss playing with you. Isn't that right, Michael?"

"That's right," Longbow agreed, shaking his head. "There was no better piece of ass on this team." He came up behind Troy and grabbed hold of him, pulling the hitter back.

Troy swung out, trying to free himself, but Longbow tightened his hold.

"Sit him down," Mills ordered.

Longbow did as instructed, forcing Troy down on the bench.

Mills came up close, his stiffening cock in front of Troy's face. "Suck it!"

"You suck it," Troy spat out, and with a quick move, pushed back against Longbow enough to raise his leg and kick Mills with his foot.

The force sent both players rattling against the lockers.

"Big mistake," Mills forced out, attempting to gain control of his breath.

"For you two, that is." Troy retrieved a bat from the corner of the room. "Now if you don't get the fuck out of here, I'll show you just how well I can still hit balls."

The players traded looks. Stumbling with their balance, the two grabbed at some clothes in their open lockers and staggered out without another peep.

When they were gone, Troy dropped the bat and fell onto the bench in tears.

He was in total fear of what just happened. Not so much of being hurt by Mills and Longbow, but of the emotions and desires that were aroused in him. Troy's cock was rigid and no matter how he tried to pass it off as the adrenaline pumping through from the attack, he really knew it was from Mill's pole poking in his face.

"Are you okay?" A voice asked.

Troy turned around to find Joey Dumbfell approaching him carefully.

"What do you want?" Troy bellowed at Joey.

Joey was standing right in front of him in only a towel. He had just come out of the showers and, despite the towel's efforts, was still wet. Droplets of water streaked down Joey's baby face. The boy was only nineteen and had been picked up off his high school team. The other men used to joke that Joey was still a virgin, something the kid never confirmed nor denied, just laughed it off in the good nature the jab was presented.

"I just wanted to say I'm sorry."

"For what?" Troy stiffened up. Had Joey been witness to what just happened between him and the guys?

"I didn't sign on to take your place. That wasn't part of the deal. I had tons of teams clamoring for me to sign with them."

He exhaled in relief. "So why'd you pick this one?" Troy watched the floor in fear that his eyes might give something away.

"Because of you?"

"Me?!" Troy looked up at Joey and noticed how brilliant his blue eyes were. They beamed with excitement.

"You were like my idol. I wanted to be you. That's how I got to be so good at playing ball," he smiled.

"How do you feel now that you've out-mastered me?" His fear of being found out was replaced by bitterness. Joey's soppy confession was churning his stomach. He put aside the thought of the guys. The fact that he was about to be let go from the team because of this kid came rushing back to the surface with a force surely capable of knocking Mills and Longbow out.

"I've not out-mastered you, and I'm sure Coach doesn't think so, either."

"Since he's about to fire me, I highly doubt that."

"He's not going to fire you. I wouldn't."

"Oh? And why not?" Troy wondered if the kid was trying to annoy him on purpose.

"'Cause you're hot?"

Troy stared at Joey in disbelief and, for the first time during their talk, realized that his face was level with Joey's towel-clad crotch, which was now tenting the thick, white, soft fabric.

"Ah, look, kid, I don't know what you're thinking, but you better stop."

"I'm not thinking, I'm acting. Don't you ever want to act on your feelings, Troy? Aren't you tired of fucking around with girls because you won't allow yourself another guy?"

"Now that's going too far."

"Just give in to it. You know you want to." Joey dropped

his towel, freeing his rigid cock. It pointed right at Troy as if accusing him of a crime he hadn't yet committed.

"I may swing bats, kid, but I don't clean 'em." Troy tried to stay calm. Had Joey actually been witness to what happened after all? Were all three teammates in some sort of game together?

"Then by all means, grab hold…" Joey moved in closer, his fat, young, veiny cock inching towards Troy's full lips.

Troy swung his hand to slap Joey's meat away, but before he could even get a hit in, the newbie grabbed hold of Troy's arm.

The two players locked eyes, Joey's full of lust, Troy's full of fear, and as they continued to stare, Joey gently guided Troy's hand to his bat and balls, which Troy took hold of freely.

Joey moaned out, relaxing his body.

Troy looked from Joey's eyes to his cock. The young flesh stretched over the engorged muscle, the low-hanging, full, hairless sack. Troy was enticed. It had been so long since he let a cock slip through his lips. As soon as he made it big, he forbid himself his little indiscretion, but he never stopped craving it. If Mills and Longbow hadn't come on so aggressively, Troy might have actually bent his will to them, just as he had when he first started out on the Ballers. He looked back up into Joey's eyes. The boy was right in some way. He did keep hitting pussy as a way to quench his thirst for man meat, but it never satisfied him. Now that he was on edge already, and this kid was presenting him with a non-intimidating chance, Troy knew he needed to take it.

Jerking the long log loosely so that the skin gave with it, Troy opened his mouth. He wet his lips slightly before pursing them to kiss the bulbous head. The instant flesh met flesh, Troy was lost in desire. All his feelings from the past came rushing back just as quickly as the blood rushed through his cock, making it even harder. He grabbed on to his own wood while carefully sliding Joey's cock into his warm wet mouth.

The newbie pumped gently. Troy was in heaven. He missed sucking cock so much.

Clamping Joey's ass, Troy pushed the kid further towards his face, allowing him to take all of Joey's fresh meat. He savored every inch of the hairless beauty. Troy ran the tip of his tongue around the head's rim, sending Joey to throw his head back and moan loader.

"Oh fuck, Troy."

Troy couldn't help but smile. The boy was going to be putty in his hands.

"My balls. Do my balls," Joey begged.

Licking the right nut, then gliding his tongue over to the left, Troy bathed Joey's sack with his spit. The boy was panting heavily, but Joey had seen and felt nothing yet. Mouthing Joey's balls with his full lips, Troy scooped both nuts up into his mouth, sucking on them until Joey had to pull away.

"God, you almost made me blow my load."

"We wouldn't want that yet, now would we?" Troy grinned.

Joey just nodded and looked at Troy in lust and awe. "I've been waiting for this day since I first realized the sight of you turned my dick hard," he gushed.

"I'll try and make it worth the wait," Troy chuckled. "Now turn around and let me show you what else my tongue can do."

Grinning from ear to ear, Joey obliged.

With the boy's round, firm ass in his face, Troy had no choice but to pry those smooth cheeks apart, exposing the prize he was after. Joey's pink puckered hole was so tight and sweet that Troy dove right in, licking, sucking and fingering. He bent Joey over so he could have better access to the kid's home base. Troy shoved his face in, going mad on the boy's hole.

Joey was crazy with desire, groaning and moaning and supporting his trembling body against the lockers. He kept pushing back into Troy to get the hitter's powerful tongue deeper inside him, but Troy had something more powerful to stuff deep into Joey's dugout.

"You better brace yourself, kid," Troy instructed, pulling his face out of Joey's ass and standing up. "I'm gonna show you just how good I am with a bat."

Walking over to his locker, Troy pulled out his duffel bag and rifled through it until he found what he was looking for. Trotting back over to Joey with a condom and a bottle of sex grease in his hand, he resumed his position behind the newbie.

Spreading on a generous layer of the grease, Troy worked it into Joey's clenched hole, his fingers slipping in and out easily. Rolling on the glove and giving himself a generous amount of the grease, Troy stroked his bat before pressing it against Joey's base.

"You want this, kid?" Troy sneered.

"Please..." Joey turned his head so he could see Troy behind him.

It took a few years, but Troy was finally on the giving end of ass pounding. Mills and Longbow never let him fuck them. They just used his hole over and over again. But now it was finally his turn to give what he had once loved taking.

In one swift motion, Troy had sunk balls deep into Joey. The kid let out a small gasp. Troy eased up. He pulled his thick dark meat out and slowly slid it back in. He was going to fuck Joey nice and slow so he could savor every moment.

"I love the way your ass grips my cock, kid. You done this before?"

"No," Joey said softly. You're my first. I told you how I

felt. I've been saving myself for you."

"Oh fuck, kid, that's hot." Troy picked up some speed, led on by the excitement of this discovery. "No wonder you're so tight. Urgh," he grunted, pounding into Joey, his balls slapping against the boy.

"Feels good, don't it?"

"Fuck, yeah, Troy. Pound me harder."

"If you're sure you can take it?" Troy asked, then slapped Joey's ass.

"I want to take it."

Troy smiled and went at Joey with full force. He gripped the kid's hips while Joey gripped the metal grating of the lockers. They shook with each thrust Troy gave Joey which was followed by a grunt from Troy and a deep, lustful moan from Joey. The harder Troy pitched his cock into Joey, the louder the lockers rattled, and the louder their sounds got.

Joey was beginning to scream out. He clutched his cock and started jerking it.

Troy knew he would erupt soon, but he wanted to make Joey cum while he was still inside of him. Troy slowed down and started long dicking the kid and slapping his ass.

"Oh, God, I'm gonna cum," Joey shouted, decorating the locker room floor with his heavy load.

The tightening of Joey's hole on Troy's cock when he came was enough to set Troy off. He pulled out of Joey, spun him around, yanked off the condom, and shot a hot load all over the newbie's baby face.

"What the fuck is going on here!" Coach McNara bounded in the locker room.

The players jumped at his roar.

Coach moved in close to the guys. "So this is what was taking you so long, Rodriguez."

Troy stuttered, but couldn't find a response.

"On the bench, both of you."

Joey picked himself up from the floor and took a seat next to Troy, who was looking particularly ill.

Coach paced in front of them. "You think this is acceptable behavior, do you?"

They remained speechless and motionless.

"Have nothing to say?" He stopped pacing and stood, looking down at them. "Well, I have something that will get your mouths open." Coach dropped his pants and pulled his cock out of his shorts.

Troy and Joey stared at Coach's soft cock, not knowing what to do.

"Come on, boys. Don't go all shy on me now. Why don't you show me what good a team players both of you are?" Coach grinned and took hold of his dick, offering it to his players.

With a quick glance at each other, Troy and Joey both headed in for Coach's member.

"Oh yeah, now that's it," he moaned as Troy lapped at his balls and Joey slurped on his knob. With the two guys going at it, it didn't take long before Coach was ready to explode.

"Take it," he cried out as he blew his wad over their faces. When he was done, he took a deep breath and pulled up his pants.

The guys sat where they were, cum dripping from them.

"Go get yourselves washed up," Coach ordered. He started to walk out of the locker room, but right before he left, he shouted, "I'll see you both at practice in the morning."

Troy looked at Joey with a smile on his face.

"What did I tell ya?" Joey gloated. He found a towel on the floor and wiped his face, then handed it to Troy to do the same.

"Come on," Troy got up from the bench, pulling Joey with him. "Let's hit the showers." He slapped Joey on the ass as the two made their way to get cleaned up.

"Hey, what are you doing tonight?" Joey asked as they left the locker room.

"You," Troy beamed and pulled Joey in for a deep, hard kiss.

MAKING THE GRADE

Art by Terry Blas

Drew was not the brightest college student. He had ability, but lacked motivation. I encouraged him whenever he did his work, which was not often. The days he came to class, he would sit quietly in the back, muscles flexed, lips pursed, eyes heavy from smoking up. I would sneak glances at him, hoping no one would notice. At the end of class he would stand up and stretch, his shirt riding up to reveal a flat stomach, perfect v cut and treasure trail. It was all I could do not to see where it led. I always wondered if Drew suspected I was hot for him. He never let on, and I tried my best to seem unbothered by his sexiness. It was undeniable though. Drew was a stud: Young, hard, and built to fuck. He liked to wear thin sweatpants that showed he was packing major, major meat.

By the end of the semester, Drew was failing and I was blue-balled. On the last day of class I called him over and waited until all the other students had gone before speaking to him. I asked if he knew he was failing. He nodded, looking right into my eyes. His stare was intense and I stirred. My dick began to swell. I hadn't planned on it, but I couldn't help what I was about to do.

"Is there anything you can do to pass?" I asked, looking him over with my eyes, making sure to linger just long enough on the bulge in his sweats.

He moved his full lips to speak, but said nothing. Instead, he inched closer to me and grabbed his crotch. "I can give you this," he said slowly, "if it will help me pass." He released himself.

My heart started to beat faster as an overwhelming feeling took over my body. Could this really happen? I felt the strain of my now fully hard dick pressing against the fabric of my trousers. I swallowed hard and looked up from his crotch.

"I see you look at me," he went on. "Checking me out," he grinned.

So he knew.

"You hungry for cock, Professor?" he asked, rubbing himself. "I'll feed it to you for a passing grade."

My eyes were fixed on Drew handling his meat for me. I knew it was wrong, but I had to have it. I had desired it for months. I was more than hungry for this young guy's cock—I was starving for it.

I nodded my head yes. Drew smiled.

"We should go someplace," I finally managed to say. "Not here." I checked the door to make sure no one was pressed up against it, peering in.

"My car's in the back lot. You know which one it is," he winked.

I agreed and proceeded to gather up my books and papers as he left. Somehow I got everything in order, fumbling hands and all, and carefully placed my briefcase in front of my raging hard-on so no one would notice as I walked out of the building.

Drew was waiting in his car when I reached the back lot. He had parked all the way in the far corner. His seat was fully reclined and his legs were spread wide. He was still clothed and had just finished smoking a joint.

"Get in," he ordered. I did as told. I tossed my briefcase into the back and took my place in the passenger seat. He looked over at me, then down at his hard-on.

"Suck it, Bitch."

I obliged. I leaned over and mouthed my student's cock right through his sweats. The hardness of his cock felt good against my lips. I mouthed down the shaft and found his balls. I kissed them, licked them through the thin fabric, loving every moment of it. But my hunger for flesh overtook me and I lifted my mouth off his meat just long enough to pull down his sweats and release my prize. His cock was mesmerizing, thick and veiny with a bulbous head. He was hairy, which I liked. His balls were big, heavy low hangers, and as I took them in my mouth, I knew I wanted the juice building up inside of them.

Drew moaned. "I can never get my girl to eat my balls. I might have to come back for more," he said, rubbing my head.

I'd be happy to feed on them anytime he wanted.

Drew pulled my head up by my hair. He reached for his cock with his free hand and slapped it against my face.

"You want it?" he asked between slaps.

"Yes."

"Of course you do. You've wanted it for a long time." He teased my lips with the head of his cock. "You should have asked for it the first day of class. I wouldn't have had to come so much." He slipped the head in my mouth then took it right back out. I was busting. The boy knew control. "Maybe I won't give it to you after all." Drew pulled my head up far enough so I could look at him. He had a sneer on his face which almost made me shoot my load.

"Say please."

"Please," I said gently and began to rub myself. The pressure building inside my pants was getting too much.

"I can't hear you. Say please."

"Please." This time I said it louder.

"That's more like it, Professor Faggot. Now choke on it."

Drew forced my head down and rammed his cock into my mouth. The girth of it alone was hard to contain, but he kept holding my head down while arching himself up so his cock would go deep down my throat. I gagged a bit at first, which he seemed to get off on, but my willingness to please him took over any gag reflex that existed. I sucked on his cock with everything I had. All those weeks of desire and I was finally slurping on the meat I had dreamed about.

Drew moaned heavily as I deep-throated that fucker, and pretty soon he released his hold on my head, letting me go at it on my own. I could feel his balls tighten against my chin and I knew Drew was about to offer me dessert. I gave his shaft one last deep-throating before rising up to suckle on the fat head. He let out a loud grunt as his cum began to flow. As soon as I tasted his juice I dove back down and took all of his cock, down to his balls, letting Drew's cum empty into my stomach. It was enough to make me shoot my own load in my pants.

When he was empty, I cleaned his cock for him and sat upright in my seat. He looked over at me with those heavy eyes and cocky smile. "So what'd I get?" he asked.

I looked at the cock I just drained. It really was huge. "Oh, I think that was a 'C+'," I said casually. He looked at me funny. "But I can tell you what you can do for an 'A.'"

GETTING WHAT HE WANTS

Art by Alan Ilagan

I knew it would be difficult for me to live in a frat house for two reasons. One was that I was waifish and nerdy while most of the brothers were buff and jockish, and the other was that I was very quietly gay, but I pledged anyway because I always wanted that type of college experience. It was my first semester as a sophomore, and I had been living in the house for a month after pledging the end of my freshman year. So far things had been going well. I was able to make it through hazing in spite of all the drunken, naked frat boys, curbing my urges by whacking off in the showers, which weren't exactly private, so I had to be quick about it. I would work up a good lather and work my cock and balls to the image of my frat bothers' cocks. There was a good variety to fantasize about. Some were average, but there were a few that would give the paddle a run for its money. The image that always got me to lose my load was of one of the brothers slapping me across the face with his "meat paddle." I would have to brace myself against the shower wall as my jizz pumped out of me, coating the stall.

Because I was a newbie, I was roomed with one of the big brothers named Devon. He was a junior and a pretty okay dude. Quiet, but presented just enough of a hint of that don't-mess-with-me persona to know not to mess with him. There was something else about Devon; he exuded an unbelievable amount of sexiness. I was immediately turned on by him, but kept my desire in check. He had the type of cut jaw that just makes you want to trace it with your hands, and when it was stubbled... But his jaw wasn't the only cut thing about him. Devon was ripped to perfection. He worked out in the house gym whenever he wasn't in class. Every inch of him seemed as chiseled as marble. I noticed this a lot as Devon was always in various states of undress in our room. It was hard not to sneak peeks. Once, Devon had returned to the room, exhausted from whatever he had been up to. He managed to strip down to just his tighty whities before passing out on the bed. I tried to keep my head in a book but I just couldn't. The briefs fit like they were cut for him, cupping his manhood in a presentation. But it wasn't just his package that struck me. It was the way he slept. He looked so beautiful, so peaceful. I watched his washboard stomach rise and fall with each breath. I wanted to curl up beside him and learn what it felt like to be in the arms of someone so sexy and so strong. Of course I couldn't take that kind of risk, but there was something I could do, even if it was wrong of me. Tossing my textbook aside, I got my camera and starting taking pictures of Devon. I was nervous that the sound of the flash would rouse him, but Devon was too far gone. I snapped away, getting images from as many angles as I possibly could. I figured these pictures would be my only chance of getting off with Devon aside from providing me with a lasting impression of his beauty. I loaded them on to my laptop and when I was alone in the room, which was often, I would flick through them, rubbing one out as I did. I did this so many times that every erotically charged image became permanently burned into my memory.

Like I said, things were going okay. I had my pictures and my shower jerk offs and the other brothers were really welcoming to me. I felt that I had made the right decision and that I could, after all, handle a house full of testosterone and booze driven college studs. And then that all changed. I had come home one day and sat down at my desk. My laptop was on. I got an uneasy feeling. Out of nowhere Devon came up from behind and put me in a chokehold. He dragged me out of my chair and threw me down on his bed. He held me down firmly with his full weight while he used his arm to crush my windpipe. He looked at me with furious eyes.

"I found those pics of me on your laptop, you fucking perv. You some kind of faggot?" he shouted.

I didn't know what to say. How could I get out of this mess? Even though I was scared for my life, there was a part of me, namely my cock, which was completely aroused. The guy I had been jerking off to pictures of for a month was on top of me. We were physically closer than ever. How could I not spring wood?

"Are you fucking hard? You are a little faggot aren't you?" Devon released me and sprung up. He paced around the room while I regained my breath.

"Wait till I tell the brothers about this," he muttered to himself, wearing a trench into our floor. He kept shaking his head and pounding his fist into his palm. "They're going to kick your pussy boy ass out of here." He stopped and looked directly at me. "That's if they don't use it first."

"Devon," I said meekly, sitting up on the edge of the bed. "I'm sorry. Please don't say anything."

Devon walked over and looked down at me. The hardness that had been in his face softened. He must have seen the pathetic, pleading look I was giving him. He remained quiet for a moment. Maybe he was feeling bad for me?

"This is how it's going to work," Devon said when he finally spoke. "I promise not to tell the other brothers if you become my personal bitch."

Was he serious?

"I need a lot of head," he went on. "Just my luck rooming

with a cock sucker." Devon cupped my chin in his hand before patting my cheek hard.

"You want me to suck you off?" I asked, still unable to believe what was transpiring.

"And whatever else I need you for," Devon winked.

"And you won't tell anyone?"

Devon put up two fingers. "Scout's honor."

I only had to think for a mere second. "Okay," I said. "I'll be your bitch."

A wicked grin spread across Devon's face. "Good boy."

I nodded and took a deep breath. I could do this. I could be his bitch. I would have willingly, but under the circumstances, what other option was there? I couldn't be outed to the house. That would not be good on any level.

Reaching out, I grabbed the waistband on Devon's jeans. I tried to unfasten the button when Devon clutched both my wrists.

"What are you doing?" he asked, shaking his head.

"You said you wanted me to blow you."

"When I need you," he said, lowering my hands. "When I need you."

A week had passed since my arrangement with Devon and he had yet to need me. I started to wonder if the whole thing was a joke—a lie, if Devon had actually told the other brothers and they were just lying in wait. I had visions of them coming for me in the middle of the night. I would be bound and gagged and tossed in the basement where they would paddle me to death. On occasion the visions switched from death by paddle to one massive gang rape. They would use me until I broke. Even though this was a fear, I always ended up hard when I thought about it.

The whole situation kept me on edge. I just needed something to happen. Whatever it was. And then it did. Two weeks after I had agreed to be Devon's bitch I woke up with his heavy meat in my face. My tired eyes took in his naked body straddling me. Before I could even utter a whisper, Devon dipped his balls in my open mouth. He jostled them in and out. It took me a moment, but once the element of surprise had passed, I started my duty as his bitch and worked his heavy sack.

"That's it," Devon moaned. "Keep this up and you'll get a big load across your face."

I mouthed his nuts harder, turned on by the idea of Devon coating my face with his cum. His cock had become hard from my juicing up his nuts.

"Take my dick," Devon said, removing his balls and pushing his fat head up against my mouth.

His thick meat slid between my lips, the head hitting the back of my throat. I tilted my head back so his cock could make it all the way down. Devon moaned as I deep throated him. My own cock was responding to my working Devon's rod like the bitch I had become. I reached for my throbbing dick to satisfy it, but before I could even get a stroke in, Devon batted my hand away.

"You don't get to stroke," he ordered, then pushed his cock further down my throat.

My cock was driving me crazy. It needed release. I needed release. I sucked Devon's dick harder and deeper. I loved having him fill my mouth, but if I was ever going to cum, I needed him to cum first.

Devon began rocking back and forth to the rhythm of my sucking. "That's it," he breathed. "That's it."

I could tell he was getting close and went in for a final deep throating I knew would take Devon over the edge.

"Fuck!" Devon shouted, pulling his cock out of my mouth just in time for him to shoot his large load all over my face.

I immediately began licking up the cum that coated my

lips.

"Let me help you with that," Devon offered, taking his spent cock and using it to push all the cum on my face into my mouth. I ate every last drop then cleaned off Devon's meat, making sure to suckle out any remaining cream.

Devon got off of me and headed for his side of the room. "You did good, boy. Keep it up and I'll give you what you really want." Devon threw on a pair of shorts and left the room.

I grabbed my cock, thinking about Devon giving me what I really wanted and came instantly.

Every morning after that, I woke up to Devon's meat in my face. I couldn't complain. I loved sucking him off and there was nothing like a cum breakfast to get me going in the morning. Still, I kept thinking about what Devon said, and more so, when he was going to give it to me.

One night before the end of term, Devon bounded into our room extremely angry. Even though I had been taking his jizz for weeks, that didn't make us chums—it just made me his bitch. We didn't talk much and rarely did anything outside of our morning ritual. Devon kept his distance during house events and the brothers never expected anything was going on between us because being distant was signature Devon.

"Is everything all right?" I asked, despite our usual lack of communication. Truth be told, Devon had started to grow on me. I was beginning to develop feelings for him besides lust. Sure, it was crazy, after all, the only thing Devon ever gave me was his cock rammed down my throat, but you can't help but fall in love with a guy who willingly feeds you his meat then tells you how good you were at it or how happy you've made him, can you?

Devon stared at me hard and I turned away. I shouldn't have said anything.

"Get up," he ordered.

I hesitated.

"I said get up!"

Devon didn't wait for me. He rushed towards where I was sitting at my desk and pulled me up with his full strength. He pushed me up against the back of the desk chair, the force of it shoving the chair firmly into its slip at the desk. Devon braced himself behind me, his hands still clutching my arms.

"Tonight you get what you want," he whispered in my ear then released my arms so he could yank my pants down. "Bend over," he ordered, pushing my back so I would fold over the chair.

I kept trying to turn my head and look at Devon, but each time I did it he would grab the back of my head to keep it looking down and away. I heard his buckle and his zipper and knew this was really going to happen. I wanted to say something, not to stop him, but, like, to ask him to use lube or something, but I was terrified my talking would only infuriate him more. Devon ran a spit-lubed hand over my hole and I closed my eyes tight. This was what Devon had promised me, though I wished it would have happened differently.

Devon's fat head pushed up against my ring. I knew from blowing that cock that it wasn't gentle and it wouldn't ease itself in. No matter how afraid of his anger I was, I couldn't let him fuck me raw and dry.

"Use a condom," I shouted out, my voice full of nerves.

Devon let out a heavy moan and stopped pushing his head in my hole. I took this as a good sign and quickly yanked open my desk drawer. I rummaged around, feeling for the condoms and lube I hid there. Finding them, I raised them up in the air for Devon to grab.

My head still down, I heard the ripping of the wrapper, the fussing of latex and the squirt of the often used bottle.

Then, true to form, Devon's hefty meat impaled me. He sank himself in deep and let out a sigh of relief. He fucked me hard, remaining quiet for a good period of time. The sound of his balls slapping up against me sounded so loud. Eventually, Devon's demeanor started to change. His thrusting became more rhythmic and he began running his hands along my back and sides.

"That's it, boy. Take it like a bitch."

I pushed back to meet him, wanting to please; my cock hard and dripping more than it ever had. We got into a groove and pretty soon it wasn't just Devon fucking me. It was us having sex with each other. I didn't think it could get any better, but Devon did something that surprised me. He leaned in close and started kissing my neck and shoulders. His kisses were soft and sensual. I dared to turn and look back at him and when I did, Devon moved in and kissed me hard and passionate; his full lips conveying urgency. I kissed back.

Devon wrapped his arms around my stomach and straightened me up. He stayed inside me as we stood embraced, making out. It was amazing. Devon started a rhythm again and we fucked standing up while our tongues explored each other's mouths and Devon's hands explored my body. Every inch of flesh he touched tingled. When he found my waiting cock, Devon wasted no time in wrapping his strong hand around it. He jerked me off as he fucked me. The intensity of the situation was too much to handle. I wanted this to last forever, but I was on overload and I knew I wouldn't be able to control myself any longer.

"I'm going to cum," I whispered between kisses.

Devon responded by thrusting his cock inside of me harder and deeper. He put a firm grip on my dick and used short strokes as my cum erupted out of me. I felt Devon tense up and I knew he was cumming with me. I kissed him as hard as I could and when it was all over we stayed connected, braced up against the chair, spent.

That night I slept in Devon's arms, my head resting on those massive pecs, arms draped across his hard body. Devon had been so tender towards me after we had sex. We actually talked, I mean really talked for the first time all semester. We forged a connection that night and I fell just a little bit more in love with him than before. I knew Devon and I weren't going to be boyfriends. He wasn't gay, and that was okay. Even though I started out as a mouth for him to use, we would end up as lovers until it was time for him to graduate. Of course, I didn't know this for sure at the time. My mind raced with ideas that maybe none of this would last and things would go back to the way they were before Devon found those pics I took of him on my laptop. What I did know was that I didn't want to continue to think about it. I just wanted to live in the moment. I curled tighter up against Devon and smiled. He didn't know it, but this was what I really wanted.

CHUB*STR*

Art by Terry Blas

The world of online dating, chat room hookups, and cybersex was not uncommon to me. I had matured during the age of advancing technology and, because of this, I seldom connected with another guy in a bar or other public social settings. So when the world of smart phone "dating" apps sprung into existence, I had no problem making use of them. The problem I did have was that in the time since I began finding men to have sex with over the Internet, I had gained not only years, but weight. I would not consider myself fat, I for sure am not obese, but a few extra pounds here and a few extra pounds there added up to a chubby existence. Add that to my advancing age and online hookups where becoming almost extinct. These "dating" apps were full of headless torsos so ripped, one might mistake their bodies for detailed maps of city ordinances. "It's straight up from the belly button, then hang a left at the second abdominal." Needless to say, a shirtless picture of me would scare away any visitors who preferred city living to the hills and dales of my undeveloped stomach. Still, I reasoned that a really good, deliberately posed-for photo of my handsome and charming self would get me a few interested parties. I could not have been more wrong.

What I found when I tried to connect with guys in my area was either the blatant ignorance of my, "hi" or the cut to the chase, "How much do you weigh? / Do you have any full body pics?" interrogation of my oh-so-carefully-crafted profile photo. Being a good sport, and really horny, I always obliged as best I could, which always turned into these men blocking me or simply going silent. It was diminishing. I felt terrible about myself. Unwanted, undesirable, and washed up. I surely thought I would never have sex again. I allowed my self-worth to be stripped away by a legion of over worked-out twinks whose vanity rivaled the person Carly Simon wrote that song about. Of course they didn't want me, they wanted themselves. Those boys on the apps wanted nothing more than to fuck mirror images. And by all means, let them. I just wasn't going to be the one to tell them that one day that mirror will crack. My understanding of this did not happen right away. It took some time, some failed attempts at still trying to connect with the torsos, and a friendly comment by another older, more average-bodied guy who was just "looking to chat."

"Try chubstr," he messaged me.

"What's that?" I queried back.

"It's for bigger guys and their chasers."

There it was. I was officially exiled to that gay subculture known as Chubs. Chubs were gay men who were fat, not huge, but not muscly or gruff and hairy like bears or cubs. Those were the Chubs' cousins and often attended the same outings. I hated to think of myself in that way, but I had to be realistic. I had become a bigger guy, and if, as a bigger guy, I ever wanted to have sex again, I needed to go where the bait was. I downloaded the app to my phone, set up my profile— chub-friendly pic included—and waited for the chasers and fellow CHUBstrs to come and find me. I was inundated. Guys from all around my area and farther were either messaging me "hi"s or sending me "mmm"s, CHUBstr's way of allowing a user to tell another user "you're hot" in a coy manner. I was very excited to say the least. But my excitement faded when it became apparent that most of these guys were dead ends, time wasters, picture collectors. We messaged dirty, but none of them had any intention of following through. I just could not understand it. Were men that satisfied with jerking off? Yeah it can help, but I'm sorry, I needed real action to quench my lust.

A few weeks into using CHUB*str* and I was ready to delete this other damn waste-of-time app from my phone. I figured there was no hope for ever having sex again when I got a notification that someone named boi4chub sent me an "mmm." I opened up the app and checked out the user's profile. I was stunned. This young male with piercing brown eyes and over styled hair looked right into me through his customary bathroom mirror selfie, which had become the norm for these types of "dating" apps. He, of course, was shirtless and ripped. His body was very slight, not an ounce of fat on him, and trim in the way young guys are today: Lean and gaunt with a waist size that rivaled any 12 year old girls'. What the fuck did this kid want with me? According to his stats he was:

Location: 5.2 miles away
Ethnicity: White
Age: 19
Identify As: boi, chaser, bottom bitch
Looking for: daddies, chubs, bears
About: yng boi lookin for older dudes 2 use me good love bigger guys who can dominate me an make me there bitch hit me up if ur into daddy/boy fun

Well, I wasn't a daddy, and not much in the way of a "dominator," but I was intrigued.

"Hi."

"U want to use me?"

"Maybe?"

91

Without provocation, a pink, puckered hole popped on the screen. It was so fresh and clean. I knew I had to have it.

"I want to eat you out," I typed.

"Mmmmm I love a man making out with my pussy before he fucks me"

My dick sprung up in my jeans.

"Can I see your cock?" I asked, curious what other mouthwatering attributes this twink had on offer.

"I don't show guys my cock. They come over pretending they are tops then try to get me to fuck them."

"That's a shame," I sympathized, genuinely feeling bad for the boy. I could only empathize with the number of misfires he must have endured in his few short years. He might have been young, but he deserved to be fucked long and hard by a man who knew just how to make use of a sweet little pussy like his. And though it had been quite a while, I knew I was the man to do it.

"Do you get a lot of action otherwise?"

"Not as much as I used to haha

"I used to go to these 18 to party, 21 to drink clubs and while the other gay boys were getting their dance on, I was the one in the corner with an older guy fingering my ass."

My finger twitched with anticipation as I typed, "When can we meet," anxious to get my raging hard-on inside this youth.

"Today? Can you host?"

I could host, I supposed, but I often opted to go to the other guy's house. I didn't need any stalkers. Sometimes bottoms became attached.

"Can you?" I asked

"No. I live with my family."

"Ah. Do they know you take it up the ass like a little bitch?"

"Some things you just don't talk about over dinner."

This boy was funny and charming, endearing even. I was just about to tell him he could come on over when he asked,

"Will you fuck me raw?"

I stared at the message for some time. Was he serious?

"Do you often get fucked raw?" I asked, unsure how to proceed. This was new territory for me. I had never had a guy ask me that.

"Only if a guy takes it. Then I get bred. If he asks I say no."

There went the endearing quality and my hard-on. But some other feeling was taking root. Worry. I was concerned for this boy. He was young, only 19, and was allowing strange older men to "take him" and cum inside his beautiful boy pussy. I mean, I could totally see the appeal, but I knew it wasn't right, or safe.

"Are you clean? Do you get tested?" I typed in hurriedly.

"Every two months"

"It should be every three months," I replied. Didn't he know this?

He went quiet and I thought for sure I had lost him, that I had scared him away with my talk of STD testing. And not that I wanted to sound like a PSA, but the kid had to know about being sexually responsible. Back in my youth, no one dreamed about bare-backing. AIDS was still a major part of my generation's reality and it was talked about and discussed in ways it no longer was. Which made me think, were youths like this one taking it raw because they thought the threat of diseases had been diminished simply because no one hammered on about it any longer?

I didn't have long to contemplate that thought because, for whatever reason, the boy messaged me back.

"So are you going to fuck me?"

I hesitated. My cock was saying yes again, but my mind wasn't so concrete.

"You know I'm a big guy, right?" I asked, stalling.

"Yeah"

"And you're sure you're okay with a larger man? You're so fit."

"Stop trying to turn me off you. It's not going to work. This is chubstr and I'm a chaser."

A chaser, huh? Maybe in more ways than one.

"Yeah," I keyed in against my better judgment. "I'll fuck you, but not raw."

"cool"

"Cool," I wrote back.

I gave him my address and he said he'd be over in a half-hour or so. I set my phone aside and started to prep, which meant showering down and tidying up. The whole while a little voice in the back of my head taunted me that he wouldn't come, and as thirty minutes turned to forty and forty turned to sixty, I was beginning to believe the boy wasn't going to show. I was ready to chalk it up to another stupid fake-out and jerk-off my frustration when the doorbell rang. It was what I had been waiting for, but it crept up on me in such an unexpected fashion that I jumped at the shrill. Taking a few deep breaths, I opened the door and found the sexiest boy ever to cross my threshold. He looked hot in his pics, but in person he was steaming. His jaw, cheekbones, and nose were long and sharp, his heavy brown eyes deep set. His whole face had an expression of forlornness that seemed to be so common in young men these days. He had more hair on his head than I would ever know what do with, but he seemed right at home styling the sandy blond tufts in gravity-defying angles.

"Sup?" he asked and jerked his head in something that passed for a nod.

"Me, apparently," I said clumsily and cast my gaze down to my shorts which were at maximum tent.

The boy grinned. I led him inside my house.

"Nice place you got here," he said as we sat down on my sofa. The boy wasn't shy at all, as he eased down right next to me.

"Thanks," I said, staring at him. There was a beat, and then he yanked off his shirt revealing that chiseled, fat-free torso. I placed both my hands on my middle-age spread and said, "Are you sure you want me?"

In response, the boy leaned in and kissed me. He was a man of few words, but as I kissed him back, I didn't mind that, not one bit. As I was becoming enchanted by this boy's full, pouty lips, his hand made its way to my cock and he began stroking me through the thin fabric of my shorts.

"What's your name?" I asked all breathy between kisses.

"Riv," he said, equally breathy.

Very hot name, I thought.

"What's yours?" he asked.

"Barry." Not hot at all.

"Take your shirt off," he said, tugging at my t-shirt.

After all my bad experiences on those "dating" apps concerning my new, chunkier body, I would normally have hesitated to reveal my hairy belly and spare tire to a fine specimen like Riv, but between the heavy kissing and the light stroking, I was in too deep to care.

"Here," I managed to get out during the minuscule parting of our lips, and helped him remove my top.

Riv grinned as he took in my bare chest and middle. He ran his hands over my chest, lightly playing with my body hair, then circling his finger around each of my nipples before drawing that finger from my sternum down my torso and finally to my pillowy stomach, where he circled my bellybutton. Scooching down, he kissed it. Not some cute little peck, but a full-on tongue and lips kiss. I had no idea what this tight teen found desirable about my middle-aged spread, but whatever it was, it sure turned him on.

Looking up at me with a wide smile, Riv slunk back up and maneuvered his slight, but oh-so-tight body into a straddle position on my lap. My bone was pressed hard into his denim-covered ass, but it was the inside of this demi-god that I really wanted my cock pressed hard into.

With our arms wrapped around each other, Riv rocked back and forth in my lap while I ground my crotch up and down to meet his movements. We kissed pretty steadily, every so often Riv allowing a soft moan to escape those sexy lips of his. And just when I thought I couldn't contain myself any longer and I was going to have to rip my boy's jeans right off and bury myself in him for real, Riv stopped dead and slid off of me. My heart stopped; my face a mixture of frustration and confusion. What had happened?

My mouth must have been hanging open from the abruptness of it all because Riv looked at me and said, "Let's put that mouth of yours to good use," then slowly turned around so that his back was to me and, ever so teasingly, removed his jeans to reveal an ass so plump and firm, cupped proudly in the straps of a jock.

Kicking off his shoes and stepping out of his jeans, Riv spread his legs shoulder-width apart. He turned his head to look back at me and winked. "Get me ready, sexy," he said, then licked his juicy lips. With that, Riv dove forward, grabbing his ankles with his hands and revealing that perfect, pink pucker I had fell in lust with on CHUB*str*. Tight, smooth, and hairless, his hole beckoned me. And just like the snacks that had turned me into a chub, I knew I wouldn't be resisting this sweet treat.

Doing my own diving, I buried my face between those mounds of flesh. He smelled fresh, which I liked, and appreciated, and when I took my first lick, it was like suckling nectar. I lapped my tongue over and around his hole, switching on and off to sucking on that bud. I knew I was teasing the boy before I really went to town on his ass, but I wanted him to feel what I had felt when he was riding me with his jeans on. I kept licking and sucking and then gently flicking the tip of my tongue in the heart of his boy cunt. Boy, did that start him going. Moaning, thrusting back to meet my tongue, begging for me to open him up. I couldn't deny this cock-hungry bottom anymore. Hell, I could deny myself anymore.

Using my hands to spread his cheeks more and spread that tight port a little more open, I began to work my tongue deep inside. I was going to ready this hole for the fucking that I was more than due for. When I thought he was wet and loosened up enough, I pulled my face out of his ass, took a depth breath, and snapped the waistband of his jock. Riv righted himself and turned around to face me. His youthful cock was solid as a missile and positioned right at me through the strained fabric of his jock. Releasing it from its captor, I could see why bottom guys masqueraded as tops just to get at his delicious meat. He was about seven inches and thick with a full, pink head. A dusting of blond pubes decorated the base while a river of precum iced the tip. I stuck my tongue back out so I could lick all that sticky goodness up. Riv smirked while I lapped away at him, and once I was done, he playfully pushed me backward on the couch. My own cock was ready to rocket off through my shorts.

"Give it to me," Riv said, leaning over me and riding the left leg of my shorts up enough so that my meat poked out through the wide end.

I grabbed him in response and pulled him onto me. Riv placed his knees on either side of my hips. Reaching behind himself, he took hold of my pulsating prick and started to guide it into his well-eaten ass. He kissed me hard as he sank himself lower onto my lap. I could feel my head brushing his wet hole. The little cunt was trying to get me to fuck him raw. Though my mind protested, my body was all for it. I wanted nothing more than to have this tight, hot, young guy feed my raw dick into his willing ass. But I knew better, in spite of all the lust coursing through my body, and so I pulled Riv off my lips to protest.

Holding him away by both arms, I said, "We are not bare-backing."

Riv pouted. "But don't you want to own me?"

"No," I said, coming out of the fantasy real fast. "I just want to fuck you. Safely," I added. "And you should want that too."

Riv didn't say anything for a moment, and then, "Fine. Get a condom."

I reached into the pocket of my shorts and pulled out a rubber. I had slipped one in before Riv showed up at my house just in case we never made it upstairs to the bedroom where I usually kept them. When I pulled the package out of the nightstand, I had to inspect the expiration date because it had been that long since I needed to use one. I said a quick prayer that it hadn't been *that* long. It hadn't.

"You want to roll it on?" I asked Riv, offering him the latex.

Riv hesitated for a moment, then shrugged and said, "Sure." Without getting off me, Riv twisted himself halfway and rolled the rubber onto my cock. He may have not found it sexy, but I sure did. The sensation of his hand working the condom down on my thick six inches got me right back in the mood. I was going to fuck this tight-body good and hard. Seeming to me that he liked his tops to be "dom," I decided I would at least try to give him that much. After all, I wanted him to enjoy this as much I was, and realize that sex could be just as fulfilling with protection.

"Sit on it," I ordered, looking the kid right in the eyes.

"Yes, Sir," Riv answered with a smile, then did as he was told.

My heart was beating so fast, I could barely believe this was finally happening. But I didn't have time to think about how long I had gone without sex because the head of my wrapped cock was pressing right in the center of that pretty pucker. Riv sank down and I bulls-eyed right on through. His hole welcomed me most gratefully, letting me in without any resistance. He slid down slowly, about half way, the warmth and tightness sending waves of relief and desire through my entire body. I thrust my pelvis upward so that the rest of my cock was buried balls deep in him. Riv grunted and arched his back.

"That's it," I said, basking in the delight of being fully submerged inside this twink. I stayed perfectly still for a moment, wanting the feeling to last forever, but I also knew that the feelings that were about to come next were just as intoxicating. "Now, ride it," I commanded. "Ride me." And like a seasoned pro, he began to writher up and down my shaft, rocking his hips back and forth.

I began to meet his rhythm so that we were both in motion, making for a deeper fuck.

"Fuck me harder," Riv called out. "Fuck me real hard."

I may have become a chub, but I sure hadn't lost my touch.

Grabbing Riv around the neck, I pulled him down for a kiss. I loved making out with a guy as we fucked, and with those luscious lips, I was sky high. The harder and deeper we kissed, the harder and deeper we fucked. I didn't want any of this to end, but I knew I wasn't going to be able to last long. As sad as I was to do it, I stopped kissing Riv and pulled completely out of his ass.

"Finish me off with your mouth," I told him, breathing heavy. "I want to blow my load all over your pretty face."

Riv climbed off of me and got down on the floor between my legs. Licking his lips, he looked right at me, never removing eye contact as he moved to suck me off.

I yanked the condom off my well-worked cock and let him have it. "Don't forget the nuts," I instructed, lifting my sack up for him to lather down. "Get them nice and wet."

They were sensitive and on the verge of erupting, and Riv lapped at each ball, edging me further on. When I knew I couldn't hold out any more, I guided Riv's head off of my sack and onto my cock. "All the way down," I told him.

As soon as Riv's lip flushed against my pubes, I exploded. My whole body shook in a way it never had before when I orgasmed. But then again, I had never gone this long without man-on-man sex before. With my hands firmly on his head, I kept Riv deep-throating my meat as what seemed like an eternity's worth of cum flowed out of me and into him. This may not have been the end he wanted my seed in, but this boy was still getting filled full with my spunk. He began to gag a little and I eased up on the pressure. His eyes never left mine. A true cock-sucking champ.

When I was finally done cumming, I sighed loudly and collapsed. Riv got off my dick, but went about cleaning it up with his mouth and tongue.

"Good job," I said, completely spent, but managing to give my bottom boy a pat on the face. I closed my eyes to revel in the aftermath and must have fallen to sleep because the next think I knew, I was waking up to find that Riv was gone.

I immediately got up to search for my phone. I found it upstairs in my bedroom. Sitting down on the bed, I was still weak-legged from the nut I busted, I opened up the CHUB*str* app. As I hoped, there was a message from Riv.

"Thnx ;-)"

"My pleasure," I messaged back, then fell backwards

onto the bed. I heard the chimes of CHUB*str*'s signature message alert and smiled, thinking Riv had responded. But when I entered the message center, it wasn't from Riv at all. The "mmm" that had come through was from a handsome guy around my age.

I "mmm"-ed back at him.

"How's it going," he followed up with.

"Great," I typed out. "Really great."

BORACAY

Art by luke kurtis

"Oh Jesus fucking Christ," Carl, my boyfriend, screamed. His ass was being rammed hard by a very long, very wide cock. I knew I should be turned on, but as I watched this stranger pummel my boyfriend, I felt a mix of jealousy and doubt. Carl never bottomed, at least not for me. Now he was the bottom for not only this hung stud but for the two other guys we had invited over for a gangbang.

"Fuck yeah, fuck yeah, fuck yeah," Carl chanted while this tattooed and goateed stallion—toned, tanned and virile—made my boyfriend his bitch.

This was Carl's idea. His way of spicing up our love life which he said had become dull and expected. I thought otherwise. I found our love making romantic, the way a couple who had been together for a few years should grow into.

"Blow you?"

I pulled my eyes away from my boyfriend. One of the other guys, a young college kid I guessed, was standing in front of me naked, pulling on his cock asking if I wanted him to suck my dick. I looked down at my own soft, mediocre member and just shrugged. College boy got down on his knees and took my flaccid dick in his mouth. I watched as his full, thick lips attempted to harden my manhood. For all this blond boy's efforts it was not happening.

I looked back over at Carl, who was now being spit-roasted like a wild boar. The tattooed dude was now fucking his throat. College boy slid off my soft cock, leaving it slick with spit and got up without saying anything. He moved to the bed, where Carl was being filled to the brim. He grabbed a condom from the bowl on the nightstand and began prepping Carl's cock. I watched as College boy straddled my boyfriend, sinking all the way down on Carl's straining hard-on. There they were, the four of them, grinding and thrusting, gagging and grunting. They were in their own, getting it on and off in my bed. One thing was for certain; there was no place for me. Throwing on a pair of shorts, I left Carl to all his pig glory.

XXX

A few weeks had passed since my break-up with Carl and I had already become jaded. He had promised to love me, to spend his whole life with me, but all he really wanted was to be gang fucked on a regular basis. I no longer believed in people, let alone love. I needed to get away, to have some time alone to sort out the mess that had become my life. Winter was setting in and the thought of having to sit through another Michigan cold spell bit me hard—it's one thing to have to defrost your car, but quite another when you have to defrost yourself. I hoped that going somewhere to relax and refresh myself might be the perfect cure.

I had moved to Michigan because of Carl—for Carl— though I had my own career, which meant I couldn't just up and leave, but I could sure as hell go on a long vacation. I didn't want to go just anywhere, however; I wanted to go someplace different, someplace really exotic and very far away from everyone, especially my lying, cheating, gangbang-loving bastard ex. Distance was key.

"Someplace far," I lamented to my neighbor, Sylvia. She was rough around the edges and at most times very upfront and outspoken, but at the moment the only friend I had. Sylvia also happened to be a former travel agent back when people still used travel agents. Though retired, the old gal sure knew how to land the best travel deals.

"How about the Philippines?" she asked, a cigarette, bracing a long line of ash, dangled from her mouth.

"The Philippines?"

"You said you wanted to go far, that's pretty far," she informed me in her raspy voice. "Besides, I know of this great package deal—an all-inclusive on Boracay Island. You'll love it. White sand beaches, tanned islanders, plenty of action to keep you...distracted. How about it, Kid?" She eyed me encouragingly then fetched an old brochure to entice me even more.

I only had to glimpse it.

"Done!" I said. "How soon can I leave?"

"Leave it all to me, hon, and you'll be gone before you know it."

By the time my plane began its descent upon Manila International Airport, I couldn't wait to begin my vacation. More so, I couldn't wait to be on land again. Almost twenty-four hours in the air and I was ready to parachute out of the plane.

Sylvia thought it would be a good idea to take a boat across from Manila to Caticlan, the main port of entry to Boracay. Because these boats from Manila's port left about once a week, I had the chance to spend a few days in the capital city. The experience of the busy, creative, crazy Filipino lifestyle left me in total awe. The sightseeing opened my eyes to a world economically less fortunate than mine, but where human interaction was far more valued. It forced me to think when it was that Carl and I stopped interacting as a couple, when he stopped caring about me as a person. And everything I saw, from the twin towers of Manila that kissed during the 1990 earthquake to the ornate San Agustin church in the walled city of Intramuros, was a source of wonder and reflection. I came this far to put Carl behind me, but so far all I could think about was what I lost. This city was packed with people, and I felt like a single soul. Still, I was almost saddened when the time came to leave Manila and continue on to my island escape.

The boat ride to Caticlan was peaceful. Once we reached the island, the other passengers and I were ushered on to another boat, or *bangkas* as the locals called them. We reached our destination in a very short time. As soon as we stepped on land, we were met by a mix of tour guides and vacation guides who placed a lei on each of us and provided mango shakes to drink. A handful of us found our vacation guides, two native islanders who greeted us with a big smile and a familiar cliché: "Whatever happens in Bora, stays in Bora." This was met by knowing chuckles and a few well-meant grins.

It didn't take very long to reach the beachside resort and by the time I had checked in I was feeling a million miles away from my heartache. From my bedroom window I could see the expanse of white beach. There was nothing that compared to the sight of crystal clear turquoise water hitting white sand then trailing back to the ocean. A warm, humid breeze rustled the palm trees while a hint of salt hung in the air, enticing my senses. I took a deep breath and felt an inner calm that I hadn't felt in months. I also felt ready to explore.

There was plenty to do on Boracay. Everything from Kiteboarding and volleyball, to shopping and boating. I could scarcely decide what to do first. Having only a few days on the island, I tried to pack as much into my first day as possible. By late afternoon I was exhausted from beach activities and welcomed the palm tree-lined strip of *D*Mall* with its multitude of shops and eateries. Ducking into an out-of-the-way café, I enjoyed a scenic view over a very satisfying dish of *adobo*.

Sitting in the café, all I thought of was how I could lose myself on this island. Maybe even find a sexy Filipino to help distract me from complicated relationships. It would have been ideal. Sun and sand, buff and tanned—what more could a jaded gay boy from the chilled Midwest ask for? As I rose from my seat, ready to leave, I felt something give within me. I was feeling a bit more open and hoped that meant the healing was beginning.

Exiting the café, I collided with a very toned, very tanned, very hot islander.

"*Kumusta*," he said, smiling at me.

I shook my head slightly and gave him an "I'm confused" look.

"*Kumusta*," he repeated. "It's hello in Tagalog, my language."

My eyes widened in understanding. "*Kumusta*," I offered back, trying very hard to get the pronunciation right.

"Not bad for a beginner," he winked at me, a sparkle in his dark irises. "I'm sure I can teach you a few other things..." he trailed off, looking me up and down.

My face flushed and shyness suddenly overcame me. It had been a long time since a man, and a very attractive one at that, hit on me so forwardly. I stuttered foolishly, not knowing what to say. I wanted to respond to his advances, to indicate I was interested in learning more from him, whatever it was he had to teach me, but all I could get out of my mouth was, "I need to get back. It's been a long day." I could have shot myself then and there. What the hell was I thinking? A moment ago I was all ready to open myself up to the possibility of some island adventure and now that the opportunity presented itself, I let it slip through my fingers! I had to rest? For Christ's sake. Maybe I was in more need of help than I thought.

He gave me a bemused look and said, "Well, this island can wear you out. I'll be out tonight. Maybe I'll catch you then?"

I nodded silently, still unable to utter an appropriate and much needed word.

"I'm Paolo by the way," he said and slipped past me into the café, giving me another one of his glorious winks.

When I stepped outside, I melted, not from the immense heat that rose up from the late afternoon sun, but rather from the heat of my islander and the lifeline he had thrown my way. The whole walk back to the resort all I could do was play the scenario over and over in my head, each time changing the ending to where I was not a total flop and took him up on his offer. In these happier scenes, we ended up on the beach exploring each other's bodies with our hands and mouths, him teaching me the Tagalog words for each body part as we explored them.

In reality, I plopped down on my bed, imagining what it would feel like to be wrapped up in Paolo's arms. The images I conjured of my tanned and toned islander heated me up inside. Despite the air-conditioned room, I started to sweat and began undressing. I unbuttoned my shirt first, liking the feel of the silk fabric slipping off my chest. I ran one hand over my pecs, tweaking my nipples as I undid the buckle of my belt with the other. Moaning softly, eyes shut tight, head turning side to side, I undid the top button of my shorts and slowly brought the zipper down. Wriggling out of the confining fabric, I spread my legs wide and rubbed my hardening cock through my tight briefs. It wanted relief and I wanted Paolo.

The more I fantasized about being pressed up against him, the harder and harder I rubbed. Slipping both hands under the band, I wedged my briefs down and freed my pulsating cock. My balls were tight and ready to show the fantasy Paolo just what he was capable of producing. I cupped my nuts firmly and began to stroke my dick hard. My moans grew loud and my eyes were now shut so tight, I didn't think it was possible to open them ever again but I didn't care. As long as the image of my mysterious islander climbing my palm tree was burned on my lids permanently, I'd be happy. My fantasy Paolo wrapped his firm thighs around my waist and rode my cock like a wild buck, his sweaty muscles glistening in the sunlight. It was a picture of perfection; hotter, steamier, and hornier than any real sex I've had in a long time. I was overwhelmed by the thought, the image, the desire of it all. A powerful surge ran through me. Intensely, unexpectedly, I erupted. Cum gushed out, overflowing down my shaft and over my hands, creating a puddle of relief on my stomach. Exhausted, I drifted off to sleep, my dreams picking up where my imagination left off.

The relaxed mood I had worked myself into began to alter as I chastised myself for passing up the opportunity when I had the chance. I had lost the opportunity with my island hard-body as our paths didn't cross that night nor did they cross the day after. I tried to reassure myself by believing that letting this one go wasn't the end of the world nor was it the ruination of my vacation. There were plenty of scorching men around and if I really wanted to find some heated action, all I had to do was step out of my resort and into the right nightclub. But despite my own personal pep talk, and copious amounts of well-built Filipino lads I came into contact with night after night perusing the club scene, I couldn't help but feel a tinge of regret and an even greater swell of lust for Paolo. I wanted what I lost, and therefore what I couldn't have.

My last night on Boracay I went out again, roaming the strip, floating in and out of bars in hopes of coming across my fantasy. I was ready to chuck it in for the night and head to bed in a sullen state when I heard a familiar voice.

"*Kumusta,*" Paolo said, coming around a corner, wearing only some light shorts and a tank top. He was barefoot.

"*Kumusta,*" I confidently replied back, a huge grin on my face.

"Where have you been?" he asked, sounding disappointed that our paths hadn't crossed earlier.

"Looking for you," I admitted. I wanted him to know that this time I wasn't going to let him escape. "You're a hard guy to find."

"If you look in the right places, I'm around," he smiled, giving me a knowing glance.

"Where are the right places?"

"Mmm, come with me and I'll show you." He offered up his hand and I gladly took it. Our fingers interlocked and that feeling of being gently caressed ran up my body. His grip was strong, but not overbearing, and his fingers gently grazed along mine as he led me to his private piece of heaven.

I kept quiet as he drew me along the beach, the moonlight illuminating our path before we veered off the long stretch of white sand into a secluded area crowded with palms.

"This is my favorite place on the island," he spoke softly, bringing me down with him onto a patch of powdery white sand that gleamed in the moonlight.

"It's beautiful," I breathed. We seemed to be nestled so far away from life, save for the expanse of starry sky floating above us.

"You're tense," he said, removing my t-shirt and rubbing my neck, shoulders and back.

"It's been a tough time," I explained, going into some

detail about what brought me to Boracay Island.

He kissed my shoulder softly, his hands roaming down the side of my body to my waist. "You see," he began, his hands tentatively undoing my zipper, "We Filipinos love fully and passionately." Paolo kissed me again, this time on my neck, suckling my earlobe. "And we also give great massages." He pulled out my hardening cock from my undone pants and began to show me exactly how sensual his touch could be.

I moaned in his ear, my back arching against his built chest. We kissed feverishly while he used both hands to work over my tender balls and pulsating prick. This was the real release I needed from all the hurt and anger I had let build up inside me. I was ready to explode, my entire body bursting with desire.

Twisting our bodies, I was able to get on top of my islander, removing his tank top and flimsy shorts as our mouths kept each other busy. Black wisps of hair peeked out over the top of a fat, dark and very hard cock. My lips glided down his smooth chest and stomach until they reached the prize they were after. Taking him fully in my mouth, I pleasured him while at the same time losing myself to the wonders of this exotic beauty. My hand found his firm, round ass, rubbing it, exploring it. Spreading his bronzed cheeks apart, I slipped my thumb inside Paolo. His moistness deepened my lust for him, igniting an old desire that had died out with my ex. I knew I had to have more than a few fingers in him.

Turning my face back up to his, our eyes locked as I positioned myself to enter him.

"Do you have any protection?" I asked, eager to do what my ex never let me.

Paolo nodded. He searched for his shorts with his free hand and pulled out a condom from his pocket. He grinned as he handed me the rubber.

I plunged in, stuffing my hunk with more than my meat. I filled him with all my hopes and dreams for the future, knowing that he had not only set me free, but had started me on my real adventure—one that found me wiser, more confident, and with the ability to move on.

There, under that moonlit, star-filled Pacific sky, I took Paolo in a multitude of positions. I couldn't get enough of his tight, warm chute. The feel of his hard body fired me up even more. My desire for him was in full throttle and with every angle I filled him deeper. On his back, on all fours, on his side, on top, on bottom. I couldn't get enough. After what seemed like an endless night of intense sexual gratification, I finally came, coating my islander's well-used body. I was spent and ready to lie with Paolo for a while before heading back to my hotel, but my islander had other intentions.

Paolo wanted to return the favor and without any hesitation, I let him. Paolo was gentle with me at first, nestling into me on our bed of sand, but soon he had me up against a palm tree, drilling me savagely. I grabbed hold of the palm as my body shook from the force of Paolo's pounding. Our bodies firmly pressed against each other, heat surged through me as he nibbled on my ear. He became more aggressive and bit down on my shoulder and back. I wanted to turn around and kiss him, let him feel how much I was enjoying him, but he wouldn't let me. He secured me in my position, letting me know that he was now the one in control, nearly sending me over the edge.

I didn't think I could lose myself in his solid arms any more than I already had, but there I was, falling deeper and deeper into his touch, his thrusts, until finally we collapsed in unison, wet, sticky and warm in each other's tender embrace.

I woke up to a rising sun alone, spent, and fulfilled. Paolo was gone. Scarcely able to move, I fought my exhaustion and got myself dressed. I thought about my islander on the way back to my hotel. I would have loved the chance to say a proper good-bye to him and to thank him for all he had done for me, but, like the past that had bound me before connecting with Paolo, he had disappeared into the night.

When I got back to my room, I quickly showered and gathered up what I had yet to pack, tossing it hastily into my luggage. My flight back to the mainland from the island would be soon.

As I strapped myself into the tiny carrier that would bring me back to the great city of Manila where I would board an even bigger plane home, I knew I would never see Paolo again. I was okay with that. What we had was a magical experience only found when you search in the right places. I was extremely glad Paolo showed me where to look.

XXX

I had been back in Michigan for a few months when I ran into Sylvia. I was coming out of a coffee shop and there she was, smoking a cigarette, tapping her foot impatiently on the pavement.

"Hey," she called out in her legendary raspy voice. "How the hell are ya?" She dropped the ashy cigarette on the ground and put it out with the toe of her shoe. "You never popped by to say how you enjoyed your trip. I thought since I didn't hear from you maybe you didn't enjoy yourself.

"No, no. Nothing like that," I grinned. "Since I got back I've just been busy getting my life back together. A new man, new job, new home, you know how it goes."

"Yeah, yeah," she hacked. "So tell me, how was your trip?"

I looked at her knowingly and said, "Well, Sylvia, what happens in Bora, stays in Bora."

BIOS

Brian Centrone is the author of the mini ebook collection *I Voted for Biddy Schumacher: Mismatched Tales from the mind of Brian Centrone* and the debut novel *An Ordinary Boy*. His stories and poems have been featured in college newspapers and literary and arts journals. Four of his One-Act plays have been produced for the stage as part of the National Endowment for the Arts' *The Big Read* program. He teaches writing in New York. Visit Brian at www.briancentrone.com for more info. Follow him on twitter @briancentrone.

Terry Blas is the illustrator and writer behind the web series *Briar Hollow* and creator and writer of the comic, *Here Nor There*. His art has been used on covers for *Bravest Warriors* and *Adventure Time with Fionna and Cake*. He also contributed art to *Compete Magazine* to promote Ben Cohen's Stand Up Foundation, combating bullying and homophobia. He is the host of the pop culture examination, *The Gnerd Podcast*. He loves comics, movies, unicorns, cheese and Diet Coke. Find him at www.TerryBlas.com.

Alan Bennett Ilagan is a freelance writer and amateur photographer who resides in upstate New York. A graduate of Brandeis University, Ilagan has been published in *Instinct*, *xy* magazine, *Windy City Times*, *Q Northeast*, *Metroland*, and *Community*. He has been profiled in *Unzipped*, *Genre*, and *Upstate Magazine*. His photography has been featured in several solo exhibitions, and he served as the Gallery Manager at the Romaine Brooks Gallery in Albany, NY until 2012. He has lived with his husband Andy since 2000. More of his work may be found at www.ALANILAGAN.com.

luke kurtis is a Georgia-born interdisciplinary artist focusing on the intersection of photography, writing, and design. Self-portraiture is an ongoing element of the artist's photography as well as an interest in art/architecture, nature/abstraction, and digital collage/video. Bookmaking is a primary activity as it fuses the visual and the literary beyond gallery walls and into the hands of viewers. He has exhibited work in galleries and alternative spaces around the country. *INTERSECTION*, his debut museum solo exhibition, opened at Massillon Museum in March 2014. He lives and works in New York City's Greenwich Village. Visit him at lukekurtis.com

Rob Ordonez studied at the International Center of Photography in 2007. He has shown work in several NYC galleries, including Leslie Lohman, Munch, and Prince George. His photos have appeared in various publications, including *PMc*, *The Latino Show*, *Time Out*, *Millennium*, *Fashion Faces*, and *Vicissitude*. A book of Rob's work *LUSTROUS* is available from blurb.com. He is an aspiring actor and director with his own IMDB page. Find out more about Rob at www.RobertOrdonez.YolaSite.com.

About NLSP

We are New Lit Salon Press and we create books. We are writers. We are artists. We are makers with a mission: to publish the best and brightest, to amplify the voice of a generation lost in the void of a system concerned only about million dollar bestsellers. We look to the past but move boldly towards the future.

Founded by Brian Centrone (Publisher) and Jordan M. Scoggins (Creative Director) in 2012, New Lit Salon Press is based on the principle that Words and Art can and should coexist. NLSP is committed to publishing essays, stories, poems, novels, and art from undiscovered writers and promising artists who struggle to thrive in a marketplace that fails to recognize their talent. We believe in what you do.

The world of publishing is changing. NLSP not only recognises that but embraces it. To meet the demands of the evolving marketplace, NLSP releases are available on all major ebook platforms. However, because we are suckers for the printed page and we love the artistry of a physical object, we have teamed up with bd-studios.com to produce special, luxe print-on-demand editions of select titles.

With over 20 collective years of experience in creative, publishing, technology, and academic fields, we bring a unique skill set to the table. Our comprehensive approach is designed to nurture new and unheard talent in ways most indie publishers do not. We love what we do (and hope you do too).

We are artists. We are writers. We are NLSP and we create books.

34092594R00071

Made in the USA
Lexington, KY
23 July 2014